Life: As I See It

My E-mails to G-Ma

Jo Ann Spiess, Ph.D

Order this book online at www.trafford.com
or email orders@trafford.com

Most Trafford titles are also available at major online book retailers.

Print information available on the last page.

ISBN: 978-1-4907-8918-7 (sc)
ISBN: 978-1-4907-8917-0 (hc)
ISBN: 978-1-4907-8919-4 (e)

Library of Congress Control Number: 2018906595

Trafford rev. 06/22/2018

www.trafford.com

North America & international
toll-free: 1 888 232 4444 (USA & Canada)
fax: 812 355 4082

DEDICATION

To Twitter; a skinny tiger cat, without whom this book would not have been written.

Author's Notes

This novel is a work of fiction. However, much of it is based on factual events which have been greatly enhanced by my imagination.

The city of Naples, Florida and Lowdermilk Park actually exist. Other places and businesses have been created by the author.

All the lovely people who inhabit these pages are good friends who have freely given permission to use their names; even after reading their respective chapter.

All exaggerations and fictionalizations are entirely the work of the author.

All typographical and grammatical errors are the fault of Twitter. After all, he is just a CAT. Sending e-mails and learning correct grammar is quite a challenging feat for a small feline. He said he is still in the learning stage.

ACKNOWLEDGMENTS

I would like to thank the following for their wonderful contributions.

Many thanks to Twitter, whose antics provided the framework for this book.

There would not have been a written record of Twitter's catastrophes if son Jack, (J-Dad), had not given me a narrative of them during *his* nightly phone calls.

My husband Duane, and daughter-in-law Leslie, (L-Mom), provided invaluable help with their input by reading the early drafts and pointing out my many errors.

Many thanks also to Elliot Marks (Critical Hacker), and Elaine Ely for their critiques, suggestions, and encouragement.

Finally I would like to thank Jay Mowery for providing the perfect ending.

And lastly, I would like to thank Brenda Sutphin, Rose Kruz, and Kathy Collins. Their smiles and behind-the-scenes work was greatly appreciated.

CONTENTS

CHAPTER 1

The Midsummer Nightmares Dream

Dear G-Ma,

Midnight already and time for my nightly e-mail to you. The most horrible thing happened to me today. You could never imagine anything even close to it. It was just awful. I wouldn't wish it on my worst enemy, even if I had an enemy. Well, I could consider the huge rat terrier dog or the sneaky little green lizards to be half enemies. Anyway, there I lay on the family room carpet. My teeth were chattering because I was so cold and disoriented. At first I suspected my warm sunny spot had abandoned me. Sometimes it moves all the way across the room while I am taking long catnaps, and sometimes it even tries to hide under the television set. But then I remembered it had left me many times before during my long catnaps, and I had never gotten this cold. Apparently my warm sunny spot was not the problem. Then I thought, maybe, my long catnap had been way too long and my blood pressure had taken a nosedive.

There was no way to know it at the time, but I was definitely having an awful case of sensory and linear memory. I was almost totally unconscious and there was nothing I could do but lay there and let it all happen.

I was on my back with my four feet up in the air. My back legs were violently twitching and my front paws were madly clawing at nothing. Anyone seeing me would have thought I was either having a seizure or doing some of my fancy exercising. Eventually, even though I was almost totally unconscious and not able to control my body, I finally figured it out. I had been having a midsummer nightmares dream in the daytime. The nightmares part was due to the horrible memories of when I was younger. It didn't take a genius to know that my legs were probably reacting to the memory of my escape from death, or worse, when the big rat terrier dog chased me into the woods. Or that my front paws were reacting to the memory of trying to get up higher into the friendly tree while trying to escape from the scary black ghost; the one who came into the dark woods to murder me.

I tell you, G-Ma, when I thought I was finally awake, my little heart was doing double duty and my throat was dry from all the panting. And then a very strange thing happened. I looked around, but I couldn't see anything in the room. I couldn't see my warm sunny spot or anything that I knew was really real. I knew my eyes were open, but they were not focusing. I thought I was awake, but my vision was only replaying things from my memory bank. I was only seeing myself in former scenes and actions. It was as though I had either been transported back in time, or was watching a television program where I was the main character.

I could clearly see my first family, so long ago, in our big cozy cut-down cardboard box with the old towels in the bottom. I was so happy in our old box by the lady's back door. My pretty Mom and littermates, Gomer and Harold, were with me. I was the smallest of the litter, but my eyes had opened long before theirs, and I seemed to grow and develop faster than they did. I saw scenes of Mom and I having lots of good long talks about everything in the world. She told me all about the trains, and boats, and planes, as we heard them go passing by. And she knew about creatures and the entire outside world. My Mom knew everything about everything and she told it all to me. She even told me things that famous people had said. There were a lot of things she told me to always remember, and I promised I would remember them exactly as she had said them. I hoped all of it would fit somewhere in my little head and be there if I ever needed it.

My legs were still doing their twitching and clawing business as I continued to look around for the real world. My eyes still couldn't see anything but good memories, and I wondered how anyone could be awake and still see things that weren't there. I also wondered why my legs were behaving so crazily when I was only seeing good memory scenes.

I saw Mom as she smiled at me that one day and said, "Why on earth are you always flitting around in here instead of being calm and quiet like Gomer and Harold? You flit from one corner of our box to the other, over and around, and on top and under these old towels. Whatever are you doing all the time?"

I told her, "I'm pretending the wrinkles and bumps in these old towels are huge monsters. I crouch down for a while, and then quickly pounce on them and tussle around until I subdue them. And I pretend the ragged edges, with the loose tangled threads, are creepy crawling creatures. I have to sneak up very carefully and quietly before I pounce. Then I hold them tightly in my paws so they can't get away. Sometimes I practice jumping straight up in the air or try to twist around during a jump."

"I still haven't given you a proper name," Mom said. "I've been trying to find the perfect one for you, and now I think I have found it. I'm going to name you Flitter. You are so busy, and so inventive, and so sweet. But a kitten like you, with any other name, would still be as sweet."

"Another thing that has kept me busy," I said, "is that I need to start a security patrolling schedule here in our cozy cut-down cardboard box. One day, when all of you were taking a long catnap, a little black creature found his way in here."

"That was a new experience for you," Mom said. "What did you do about it?"

I said to him, "Who are you and what are you doing in here?"

He said, "I'm a worker ant. I scout for food. That's what I was born to do."

I told him, "I don't think the lady of the house would want you in our box too. Every time she looks in at us she says, 'I'm surely glad there aren't many *this* time!' Besides, we don't have any food for you in here. Sorry. And I'm not sure I like the idea of someone invading our cozy cut-down cardboard box."

"Okay, big shot," he said as he crawled back up the side and out over the top of our box.

"I decided right then and there," I told Mom, "to start a security patrolling business. I will have a rigid routine and will be diligent about keeping us safe from any and all unwanted and uninvited creatures."

Mom smiled sweetly at me and said, "Flitter, there is something special about you. I know what it is, but you are not quite ready to learn about it. When you grow up a little more I will explain it all to you."

G-Ma, my eyes and legs were still betraying me. I tried really hard to stop my legs from doing their twitching and pawing, and I tried extra hard to see the real things in our family room. I knew they were there, but my eyes kept seeing only pleasant memories. The only thing I could figure out, at the time, was that the good memories were going more slowly past my eyes, and my legs were way ahead of them in the memory department. *As I see it,* my legs were reacting to the bad memories yet to come.

Then, my eyes saw again that unforgettable day when one of my life-changing events happened. The lady of the house came to our box and looked inside. She did not look happy. She walked over to the back door and opened it a tiny bit. Then she walked away. Immediately I could smell new air coming in through the open door. It carried a burst of midsummer Florida's West Coast; balmy with a hint of salt, sea, and rain. This new smelling air was very intriguing.

"Mom," I screamed, "I can smell the outside air you told me about! Can we get out of our box and go out where it is?"

Mom didn't answer me because she was taking a long catnap. I didn't want to disturb her, but I needed to find out about the new smells. She had already told me all about sounds and smells, but I think I forgot it. Besides, I wanted to find out about them for myself. I stretched up as high as I could to look over the edge of our cozy cut-down cardboard box. It was no use.

The box was too high. My curiosity was on overdrive and it demanded that I do something. I was determined to get out of our box and look around outside, but I didn't want to be all alone out there. Gomer and Harold probably wouldn't go with me if I asked them, and Mom definitely wouldn't leave Gomer and Harold alone just to take me outside.

Then a brilliant idea formed in my head. I searched around in the box and found Billy. He is my favorite red, catnip, toy mouse. Billy was still under a mountain of old towels where I had hidden him from my make-believe monsters. I picked him up and threw him out over the top of our box. Then I took a big breath, and with one of my practiced jumps, I too sailed out and over the top. To my amazement, I landed on all four feet.

"Wow!" I whispered to myself, "I have just learned an amazing trick."

It seemed so natural to land like that instead of on my head. I looked around, found Billy, and gently picked him up. The door was still ajar and the new sounds and smells were still coming in from it. Quietly and slowly I crept toward the door while holding Billy securely in my mouth.

As I reached the door, my Mom awakened and called to me in a fearful voice, "Flitter! Get back here! You are too little to go outside! There are many dangers out there, and I haven't told you all about your super-danger whiskers yet!"

I paused a few seconds. It was no good. I could not go back.

Mom continued to shout to me, "Flitter, come back to the safety of our cozy cut-down cardboard box and just let life happen for a while!"

I hesitated for only a second and called back, "I don't want to sit around and let life happen to me. I want to go out and happen to life."

G-Ma, *as I see it*, when I think back to that incident, I am convinced destiny called to me more forcibly than Mom was calling to me. I felt wide awake, but my eyes were still only seeing scenes from my memories, and my legs continued to do their twitching and were madly clawing at nothing. I knew the horrible scenes were now on their way.

I saw myself standing at the back door and listening to Mom calling for me to come back. I saw myself peeking around the door and seeing clear to the end of the world! It was all so bright and beautiful! There was new stuff everywhere, and the powerful smells were inciting my curiosity. I gingerly put one paw through the small opening and pushed the door open a tiny bit more. Before I knew it, Billy and I were completely outside in Naples' wet midsummer grass.

How exciting! A whole bunch of other new stuff was waiting for me to explore. There was a wonderful warm sun that we never had in our cozy cut-down cardboard box inside the lady's house. How I wished Mom, Gomer, and Harold were there to see it. Maybe the lady would accidentally leave the door ajar again someday, and they could get out too.

I took several steps forward while still carrying Billy. The tall wet grass completely surrounded us. I could still hear Mom making a big fuss. She was saying something about my whiskers, and something about them being super-danger whiskers, and that I should pay close attention to them because they would always alert me to dangers.

Mom was making a huge commotion, and I could hear the lady of the house shouting, "What in the world is going on out here? Sometimes you cats are a big bother. Why are you making such a fuss?"

Right then and there, another of my life-changing events happened! The lady of the house looked out the door, but I don't think she saw us in the tall grass, because she slammed the door shut as she said, "Well, that's *one* less."

Her comment didn't make any sense to me, so I started to explore my new world.

Well, G-Ma, it's now time for me to make another round of my nighttime security patrolling. If all's well on all fronts, I will come back here to the computer to finish telling you about my daytime midsummer nightmares dream. And, the weirdest and scariest scenes are about to come.

Love,
Twitter

CHAPTER 2

The Chase

Dear G-Ma,

My security patrol was a short one this time. Everything was absolutely still inside and outside our house. Not a creature was stirring, not even a leaf. It reminded me of the nighttime stillness when my feline Mom thought we were all asleep. She would whisper, "All's quiet on all fronts." But I wasn't asleep. I only pretended to be asleep. If my eyes were asleep, I always kept my ears awake. She would then, somehow, slip outside for a while. When she came back, she brought some interesting new smells with her.

Now I need to finish telling you about the horrible scenes I knew were coming to my eyes, before it is time for the next security check. G-Ma, I tried so hard to open my eyes wider to try to see the real things in our family room. It was no use; the nightmare of past events continued.

I saw myself standing in the wet grass holding Billy in my mouth. "Look Billy," I said, "we can see the whole world out here. And can you smell all those new smells? Mom told me once I was good at smells. She must have known that someday I would be out here smelling all this good stuff."

Then I saw myself carrying Billy as we set off through the grass to see, what I thought at the time, would be a big friendly world filled with wonderful adventures. I made my way around the house to a sidewalk. It looked as though the sidewalk would be much easier to walk on than in the tall wet grass. I looked around and could see the big world in every direction.

It didn't matter which way I chose to go. I just started off down the sidewalk. Everything looked so interesting and inviting. We soon came to a puddle of rain water. I looked down at it and was surprised to see Billy in the water. Right then and there, I remembered my Mom saying, "Flitter, always remember, still waters aren't deep." It was a good thing to know, so I felt safe enough to put one paw in the water to touch Billy. But I couldn't touch him because he got all wavy, and distorted, and my paw got wet. I shook off the water and decided to figure out that mystery sometime later.

I walked and walked and saw all kinds of wonderful things. I recognized a lot of the stuff Mom had described to me. She told me about all the shapes of houses, and cars, and about the beautiful flowers. I was thrilled with all their colors and fragrances. I was especially happy to discover the bright warm Florida sunshine in a lot of places. I loved the sun the first time I saw it and hoped it would always be where I could find it. Something about the sun was troubling though. I couldn't understand why there was so much of it in some places, and in other places it was all lacy and splotchy, or not even there at all. I would have to work on that mystery sometime later too.

It seemed as though we walked forever, and my legs got tired. I decided to sit down, rest for a while, and just take in the new sights, and sounds, and smells. There was movement everywhere; vehicles in the street and things in the air. Leaves and tiny papers were blowing all around us. I explained to Billy it was because of a thing called "wind." It made my fur move a little, and it somehow carried smells. I wished I knew how to carry smells like that.

Billy and I rested and talked about our new adventure. I needed to explain everything to him, because he hadn't had a smart Mom to tell him all about everything in the world.

After a while, I saw what looked like a cat crossing the street, and it was heading in our direction. Its fur was much prettier and longer than mine. The wind made the fur flutter about, and the sun found its way between its long hairs. I was pretty sure it was a cat, but it didn't look anything like Mom, or Gomer, or Harold.

"Hello there," it cheerily said as it trotted up closer to us.

Right then and there, I remembered a social grace Mom told me to never forget. It was something about being assertive, and always putting your favorite foot forward. But all I could do was meekly say, "Hi."

"What's your name?" the pretty creature asked as it smiled sweetly at me.

"I'm, ah, Flitter, and I *think* this here is Billy," I stuttered. I felt the need to show off Billy for some reason. "He is my only catnip mouse red," I stammered. For some reason my brain and my mouth were not working properly.

"I am so pleased to meet you," the pretty creature said. "My name is Shirl."

I looked very closely at Shirl's lovely face. Her eyes were so pretty. I needed to say something back to Shirl, but what? What had Mom told me to never forget? I knew she told me *something* about a situation such as this, but my mind was befuddled, and my mouth was dry and tongue-tied. The silence was long and embarrassing. A few thoughts came into my head, and I tried to sort them out. Finally I uttered softly, "Are you the opposite sex, or am I?"

Shirl didn't answer my question. Perhaps she didn't hear me, or she chose to ignore my question. She smiled sweetly at me and said, "You are a young little thing aren't you? And you are very cute. I have to leave now. I'll see you around sometime later; after you grow up a little more. Goodbye for now, Sweetie." She looked back over her pretty shoulder as she walked away and added, "I hope you remember for sure if your red catnip mouse's name is actually Billy."

"Wow! That was a new experience," I said to Billy, "I was really lost for words around her."

We continued on down the sidewalk, and the wind began to blow a little harder. There wasn't as much warm sunshine anymore, and it seemed to be getting a little cooler and darker. We walked and walked, and finally came to a corner. I looked down the new street and decided to see what was going on in that direction. There weren't as many houses or cars on the street to look at, but I saw those friendly trees Mom had told me about. There were a lot of them not far away. Abruptly the sidewalk ended and turned into a dirt path.

I continued to walk and explain all the new stuff to Billy. We saw sandy lots filled with weeds and pretty butterflies. Other lots were filled with wildflowers and honey bees. "Isn't this a wonderful world?" I said to Billy. My legs were getting more and more tired, and the sky began to get darker all around us. Suddenly I felt small drops of water fall on me. I remembered Mom telling me about rain. She had said,

"Flitter, your whiskers are like an antenna. They will tell you many things, so always keep your powdered whiskers dry." But I didn't know how to keep them dry way out here on this dirt path. And maybe small drops of water didn't count as real rain anyway.

All of a sudden I was aware of a strange sensation being produced by my whiskers. Had they gotten wet and shorted out? Was I in big trouble because they had a few drops of water on them? My whiskers seemed to be sending me some kind of danger warnings. How could there be danger in this wonderful world? The signals got stronger and then the danger materialized! I actually heard it before I saw it.

It was a dog loudly barking, "Bow, wow, wow." I stopped and looked toward the sound.

G-Ma, *as I see it*, my midsummer nightmare dream was becoming absolutely terrifying. I still wonder how I lived through all those events a second time. One time was surely enough. And I knew the worst scenes were now beginning.

The loud sound was coming from a humongous rat terrier dog that was racing toward us. I stood there holding Billy; frozen in place like a statue. What should I do? Where could we hide? We were totally lost and there was no way to get back to the house with Mom. Besides, the lady of our house had closed the door. And the dog was definitely coming at us at a faster pace than I could ever run. All of a sudden I remembered something Mom told me to never forget. She had said, "Flitter, always remember, what you don't have in your feet, you must have in your head." Or it was something like that. So I told my head to think of something-anything! My head told me to remember what Mom had said about trees. So I remembered her saying, "Flitter, always remember that in a storm, any friendly tree is a port." I hoped rain drops could be counted as a storm. I was lucky she said "any" friendly tree, because I didn't have time to choose. I did wonder though, how a tree that couldn't even move could be my friend. Those friendly trees were down the dirt path, so I started running toward them. The dog was barking louder. I peeked back over my shoulder and saw that he was gaining on us!

How I wished I had never left our cozy cut-down cardboard box by the lady's back door. But it was too late for that kind of thinking. I had to protect Billy! I never even asked him if he wanted to go on this adventure with me. I just threw him up and over the top of our box and took off with him. The barking dog would tear Billy to shreds if he got hold of him.

And then it happened! I turned to peek back behind us just as the nasty dog's feet left the ground, and he became airborne. He lunged at me and I jumped aside-just in time. He didn't land on all four feet, as I had done. He tumbled around on the ground a bit, collecting his thoughts, and trying to right himself. I took advantage of his confusion and scurried off toward all those trees. I chose the first one available, held Billy tighter in my mouth, and did one of my practiced straight-up jumps. Automatically, sharp claws emerged from the ends of my paws and dug into the side of the tree. And there I stuck! Can you imagine being stuck to the side of a tree? My claws dug deeply into the tree as I hung there; still holding Billy in my mouth.

I peeked down and saw the dog right below me. "Bow, wow, wow," he barked as he jumped up to reach me. He continued to bark as he tried to jump even higher. My super-danger whiskers were saying, "Up, up, Flitter, you must try to get higher!" My claws responded instinctively to the command, and I climbed higher up the tree. I was holding Billy so tightly I was afraid I would bite him in two. The nasty dog kept circling around and around my tree and trying to jump up after me, but *his* paws wouldn't stick on the tree. He began to snarl and bare his teeth at me. My whiskers told me to hiss and spit at him.

"Ffft, ffft," I hissed at him, trying to sound like a big threat. My super-danger whiskers were saying, "Higher! Flitter, go higher!" I frantically dug my claws into the tree and climbed much higher. But then I wondered if more trouble awaited me up there.

G-Ma, the midsummer nightmares dream had my entire body reliving the horrible fright that filled me as I clung to the side of the tree. I knew Billy was as terrified as I was, and I hoped I had not hurt him by holding him so tightly.

The barking dog continued to circle my tree and try to climb it. He finally looked up at me for the last time and ran away. I let out a big sigh and looked around. There were zillions of leaves on all the trees. They were hiding my beautiful world, so I decided to get back down and figure out what to do next. But what if that horrible dog was hiding somewhere and waiting to chase me again? That was a chance I would have to take. Then horror of horrors! My feet would not move.

I told them to move backwards down the tree. They would not move. I realized we were stuck to this tree forever!

The sun wasn't coming through all those leaves anymore and a few raindrops were still falling all around us. I lowered my head and let Billy fall from my mouth to my chest. Then I hugged the tree tighter to keep him from getting wet. Mom told me there were dangers in the outside world, and this must have been what she was warning me about. Strange sounds began to command my attention. I heard a cacophony of insect, animal, and bird noises. Some creature was asking, "Whoo, whoo?" Who could that be? Maybe it was a friend who would help us.

"I'm Flitter! I'm Flitter! Who are you?" I answered. Whoever it was apparently couldn't hear me, or it didn't understand the Felinese language, because it continued to ask, "Whoo? Whoo?"

I heard other sounds too. Things were moving about in all the trees. Things were scurrying and fluttering around. What was in the trees? Were the things friendly? Mom told me birds lived in trees, but I couldn't remember a lot of I what she said. I did remember something about buzzards, and how they ate a lot of stuff. Maybe they were the ones who were making some of the noises and would come and eat me! Then, on the tree next to mine, was a creature I thought was a squirrel. I couldn't remember what Mom said about squirrels, but I shouted to him anyway. "Help, I can't get down!" The little guy looked at me and jumped to another tree limb. He looked again and jumped to another limb. I wished I knew how to do that. Then he jumped again was gone, but the scary sounds continued.

The raindrops stopped and a slight mist began to form. I could hear a dog barking somewhere. My nice warm sun was gone. The mist was creating a fog near the ground, and it started sneaking up to me. I dug my claws in deeper and pushed Billy closer into the tree. The mist and fog finally crept up and settled all over me. It even encircled my special antenna whiskers. Why did Mom tell me to keep them dry? Would they lose their power? Would their super-danger alerting abilities experience static if they got wet?

The fog continued to inch upward while making it darker around the trees. My vision began to be affected even though Mom told me I would be able to see in the dark. She said I had something called "night vision." I hoped it would kick in soon.

As I clung to my tree, I thought I could faintly see something moving. It was coming down the path in my direction. It got closer and closer. The fog had distorted my vision, but what I could see made me panic. Another one of my worst fears was materializing! Something dark and horrible was coming on the path toward me. The fog was in my eyes, but I could somehow see the thing plainly. It was creepy looking and I instantly knew it was hungry.

"Mom, Mom, help!" I shouted. I threw in a couple, "Meoooows," too. I started to cry as I screamed, "Somebody, anybody, help!" Miraculously my foggy night vision eyes saw it clearly. It was a horribly looking black ghost! I knew, right then and there, I was going to die.

G-Ma, all this remembering has me all shook up again. I need a sip of water and to do another whole house security check. Then I will finish telling you about my daytime, midsummer nightmares dream of actual events. And I'll also tell you the actual truth, *as I see it,* about that horrible black ghost.

Love,
Twitter

CHAPTER 3

The Black Ghost

Dear G-Ma,

All's well on all fronts in the household, so I'll continue telling you about my horrible daytime nightmare dream and the terrifying black ghost.

The ghost was getting closer and closer as it walked toward me through the mist and fog. I felt so helpless, and I began to cry. At first the tears were little ones, but then they became big ones. A lot of tears came as the scary black ghost got closer. My claws were even getting tired of clinging to the side of the tree, and poor Billy was getting more and more squashed. What if I fell and the black ghost got us? He would probably eat me. Or worse!

I needed to plan something quickly. Mom always said I was quick with plans and things. I continued to cry and think. I thought and thought, and finally my super-danger whiskers began to send some signals.

"Look up," they told me, "look up."

I looked up and saw a limb jutting out over my head. Going higher was not where I wanted to be. Besides, I had already gone up higher to get away from the huge barking dog.

"Up Flitter, go up higher," my super-danger whiskers told me as they urged me to go higher.

Perhaps the limb up there *would* offer more safety. I was so scared. I didn't think I could move. Eventually I *was* able to pick up Billy and move one paw. Very slowly and cautiously I reached up my paw to go higher. It worked! Up went the other paw. A few more steps up and I was able to position myself on top of a limb. I stayed close to the trunk of the tree though, because I remembered my Mom cautioning me,

"Flitter, don't ever get yourself too far out on a limb." Getting on that limb was the biggest triumph of my life. Getting away from the awful dog was also my biggest triumph. But I knew I was in deep trouble.

My teary night vision eyes could see the black ghost clearly now. I could look straight down from the limb instead of looking back over my shoulder while hanging onto the side of the tree. The black ghost was still walking toward us. Its shape looked somewhat like the lady who owned the house where we all used to live in our cozy cut-down cardboard box.

G-Ma, I tried so hard to awaken from the dream. My legs kept kicking and my paws continued to paw at nothing. The nightmare just went on and on.

"What should I do?" I said to Billy. "Should I call out for help? What if, whoever or whatever it is, doesn't like little cute kittens?" My tears had slowed a little, so my night vision eyes were seeing better through the fog. The form came closer and now looked more like a real live person instead of a black ghost. It couldn't be the lady at our house, because the person didn't have on a dress. What did this person have on? What if the person didn't hear me if I called out to it or couldn't see me in this fog and mist? But if I didn't cry out, I would surely die from hunger in this tree. I was also afraid a big buzzard bird in some tree would eat me.

Mom told me I was quick with everything, so I quickly made up my mind to call out. I also remembered Mom telling me, "Flitter, whenever you face danger, speak loudly and carry a little stick." I didn't have any kind of stick to carry, but I decided right there and then to speak loudly. Besides, my super-danger whiskers were saying, "Call out! Call out! Yell! Do it now!"

"*Meeoow,*" I loudly screamed in my Felinese language. Then I screamed a loud, "*Help!*" in the porch lady's language. I screamed in both languages over and over.

The figure stopped at the base of my tree and looked up. Through the fog and mist, my night vision eyes could clearly see that it was not a black ghost. It now looked exactly like a man dressed in black pants and a black jacket. It was quite understandable, to me, that everyone would mistake the figure for a black ghost. It was also easy for me to know, right then and there, that he was a nice man. I'm good at figuring out things like that.

"*Help*," I shouted again. "I'm way up high in this tree. Do you have night vision eyes? Can you see me through all this creeping, sneaky fog? Help me! I can't get down!"

The man looked up and said, "Here kitty, kitty, kitty." He had a nice friendly voice. "Come on down kitty," he coaxed.

I tightly squeezed Billy up against the tree and ventured one paw downward. Just as quickly I pulled it back up. How in the world was a little kitten like me supposed to know how to get down from a tree? I tried my other paw, but it came back up as fast as the first one.

"*Meeoow*," I screamed, "I'm afraid. I can't do it! My head would be looking straight down and I would fall. I can't do it! I'm too scared."

"Come on down kitty. You won't fall. Try it," the nice man said.

"I can't move! I don't know how!" I whimpered.

The man said a lot more nice things to me. I was upset, wet, and cold. And then another one of my worse fears happened! The man turned around and started to walk away. He was leaving me stranded in the tree to die and fall out. Or worse.

"*Come back!*" I shouted, "*I'll try harder. Don't leave me!*"

"My life is over," I said to Billy, "and I haven't even started it yet! My super-danger whiskers aren't helping me. I'm not even sure how they work. Maybe they are too wet to help us. They probably shorted out in all this mist and fog."

I felt very sad. And I was cold, and hungry, and lonesome, and didn't know how to get down. I had definitely learned the going up but not the going down. I looked toward the man who had been there and called out once more, "*Meeoow, help!*" But all was lost. The man was walking away.

I knew I was destined to shrivel up, turn to dust, fall down into the dirt, and blow away. "My life is over!" I said again to Billy.

How I wished to be back in my cozy cut-down cardboard box by the lady's back door. Mom always kept us warm, and the lady gave us stuff to eat. I always had someone to talk to when I was in that cut-down cardboard box on the lady's porch. I had lots of fun and lots of love there. "Now," I cried, as I whimpered aloud, "here I am, wet, cold, hungry, and dying on a tree limb." I cried and cried and cried.

G-Ma, when I was up there in that horrible situation, I remembered Mom telling me something important. It was right before one of our catnap times. She said, "Flitter, if you are ever in deep trouble, you should remember to, 'Fear not, for I....'" Then I fell asleep before I heard the rest. So, there I was, in deep trouble and didn't know what else she had said.

After what seemed like a whole night, my antenna whiskers frantically began sending me signals. "Be alert! Be vigilant," they were telling me.

It was now time to concentrate my whole attention on my trusty whiskers. My super-danger whiskers are never wrong, so I stopped crying, concentrated as hard as I could, and strained my night vision eyes to look through that creeping fog and mist.

I looked, listened, and vaguely saw it. The man was coming back, and he was carrying something big. I later learned it was called a ladder. He propped it up against my tree.

"Here kitty, kitty, kitty," he called. "Nice kitty, kitty," he continued, as he began climbing up the ladder. I picked up Billy and the man was able to reach us by stretching both arms really high. Then he gingerly picked us off the limb. I instinctively stiffened my body, but my whiskers said, "Relax, Flitter!" With that command, I immediately let my whole little body go completely limp.

The man put us in his jacket pocket and began going down the ladder. It seemed to take a long time because we were high up in my friendly tree.

When we got to the ground, he petted me and said, "You were in quite a predicament, little one. Why did you climb way up there in the first place? It's a good thing I heard you, because the fog was too thick and dark to have seen you. Stay right there in my pocket. Let's get you home." I wondered how he knew about our cozy cut-down cardboard box by the lady's back door and where to find it.

I snuggled up in the nice warm and dry pocket and held Billy close to me.

The man picked up the ladder and started walking us to our home. I knew Mom would be happy to get me back with her, and the house lady would be more careful about leaving the back door ajar when she realized I had gotten outside. I imagined how I would tell Mom all about the beautiful world I had seen, and all the things we had done. I knew she would be proud of me when she learned how I escaped from the humongous barking dog, and how I climbed the friendly tree.

I would have to tell her about my super-danger whiskers getting wet and shorting out. And how I didn't forget what she said about always keeping my whiskers dry, and I knew she would understand that it wasn't my fault. I could hardly wait to get home.

Then I sensed something was wrong. We were going too far from the friendly tree. Where was the man taking us, and what was wrong with my super-danger whiskers?

All at once I heard a horrible sound! It was a terrible sound! It was loud and creaky and spooky! Then it made a big rattling and moving sound.

G-Ma, my nightmare continued. I saw myself peeking out of the man's pocket, and a light hit my eyes. The man walked closer to the light and the awful noises started again. I stretched up higher and saw a wall coming down from the ceiling. It creaked and rattled until it hit the floor; shutting us in some kind of room. There was a car, and a truck, and lots of stuff sitting around. The man walked over to a door and walked us into another room.

"Honey," he called, "look at what I found!"

He took us out of his pocket as I tightened my muscles, squirmed, and bristled. My super-danger whiskers began telling me, "Relax Flitter, you are safe now."

A pretty lady came running and took me into her arms. "What a cute little thing. I love your stripes." She petted me and I totally relaxed. "What is this in your mouth?" she asked as she took Billy from me. "Oh, it's a red toy mouse. You both are a little wet. Let's get a nice big towel and get you dry."

She wrapped us in a towel and said to the man, "Where did you get this sweet little guy?"

"A mist started to come down as I hurried to finish my walk, and then the fog formed which made it much darker. I heard this little guy up in a tree, but it was very hard to see him. He was crying so loudly, and I tried to coax him down, but he wouldn't come down. I finally had to get a ladder to rescue him."

The lady looked at me and asked, "What is your name?"

"Flitter," I softly answered.

The pretty lady put me up to her face and rubbed my fur on her cheek. She asked again, "What is your name?"

"Flitter! Flitter!" I answered again.

"Twitter?" She said laughingly, "Are you an internet knockoff?"

It was quite obvious the pretty lady wasn't too knowledgeable about the Felinese language. Mom once told me someone famous said, "What's in a name anyway?" So, if she wanted to call me a knockoff, then Twitter would be my new name.

"Can we keep him?" she asked the man.

"Well, he doesn't seem to have a home," the man answered.

"Yes I do," I said to myself. "But I don't know where it is, and it must be a long way from here."

The lady cuddled me and said, "Wonderful, we will adopt him then."

"Wow!" I said to Billy. "Being an adoptee is one of the greatest honors in the whole world. So, *as I see it,* we are in for a heap of loving, and we will return it with our own unconditional love."

The pretty lady heated some milk and found a piece of cookie for me. We went into the family room and watched television for a long time. They took turns petting and holding me. At bedtime they found an old box in the room with the noisy door. They cut it down, found some old towels with frayed edges, and made a bed for us. I tucked Billy under one of the folds, and they carried my new cozy cut-down cardboard box into their bedroom. They put it next to their bed, and I felt very safe and comfortable.

Just as I was falling asleep, I heard the pretty lady say, "Our little Twitter has an unusual aura about him. I can't quite figure out yet what it is, but he is definitely different from any cat I ever had."

"Yes, I noticed it too. I think we are in for some interesting times with him."

Well, G-Ma, I woke up and looked around again. There I was on the family room floor. Everything was where it should be! My legs were not twitching, and my front paws were not madly pawing at nothing. Apparently I had been suffering from post-traumatic stress disorder that caused a midsummer nightmare dream in the middle of the afternoon.

All those events happened so long ago. I hope I can totally forget all the bad memories and only remember the important stuff that happened when I first became an adoptee; like giving better names to my new adopting family. As you already know, of course, your son's name is Jack, and his pretty wife's name is Leslie. But I like to keep things simple, so I renamed them J-Dad and L-Mom. Life is less complicated that way, *as I see it.*

Except for having to relive my earlier experiences, things had been going along pretty smoothly until tonight. I like everyone to keep to a routine, because I don't like changes. *My* routines are working superbly. All night I do my security patrolling to make sure no unwanted critters get into the house, and I keep vigilant in case there is any kind of disaster. During my breaks, I deliver some of my toys to J-Dad and L-Mom's bedroom door. L-Mom likes to pick them all up in the morning and return them to my cut-down cardboard toybox in the family room. I also watch the clock until it is time to get them up in the morning, and then I bump on their door a few times with my shoulder. And of course, I take a break at midnight so I can send you an e-mail about all the happenings here.

Weekends are the worse times for upsetting my routines. I am always a little frazzled by Monday morning. It takes longer to awaken J-Dad and L-Mom. They don't go off to work on Saturdays so I never know what to expect. All I can do is follow them closely to offer help and advice.

Tonight my super-danger whiskers began sending me some alert signals. We were not watching television as usual. J-Dad and L-Mom were making out lists. He was to be in charge of this and that, and she was going to do that and the other. It all made no sense to me. I was a wreck when they went to bed. How was I supposed to help them if I didn't know what was going on? My super-danger whiskers were sending stronger and stronger signals. First it was my nightmare dream and now this! I will be sure to write to you tomorrow night if I survive all this tension!

Love,
Twitter

CHAPTER 4

The Army Invasion

The disaster began early Saturday morning. L-Mom went into the kitchen and started banging around pots and pans and getting out big dishes. She started cooking a lot of stuff. J-Dad went to the garage, brought in folding tables and chairs, and put them on the pool patio. Then he took out all his loud guitar-noise stuff. I went in and out with him on every trip.

"Watch out Twitter!" he said a lot of times.

I didn't know why he insisted I should watch out so much or where he wanted me to do it, so I thought I had better stick close to him to find out.

The activity continued. L-Mom raced out to the patio with tablecloths, silverware, candles, and decorations. J-Dad spent a lot of time setting up his guitar-noise stuff. He had electrical cords all over the patio. Sometimes I got tangled up in them, and once, he too got tangled up in them. That was about the time he stopped saying to me, "Watch out Twitter!" I never figured out what the 'watch out' stuff was all about.

Well, G-Ma, I finally realized why we were doing all this activity. There was going to be a party! But then, my super-danger whiskers began warning me to be vigilant and alert for an upcoming crisis. I couldn't figure that out either, because there were lots of times when we had guests. Sometimes friends of L-Mom and J-Dad would stop by and say, "We don't have anything special to do today, and we don't have anywhere special to go. We are just at loose ends." I never saw any of their loose ends, and I wondered where they kept them.

And then it happened! L-Mom called to me in a strange tone. "Twitter, Twitter, come here quickly!"

I ran to see what she wanted. She picked me up and said, "Twitter, you are not going to like this, but it's for your own good. There are a lot of people coming, and we don't want anyone to step on you."

Before I could protest, L-Mom shut me up in the guest bedroom!

I wanted to be at the party! I was curious to see if any of the guests had those loose ends. My feline Mom said to me once, "Flitter, curiosity killed the cat." Maybe L-Mom knew about curiosity and didn't want me to get stepped on and killed.

So there I was; locked in the bedroom in solitary confinement. No way to get my little sips of water. But, someone was thoughtful enough to put my litter box over in one corner. I could see what was happening on the patio if I pushed aside one of the slats of the Venetian blind on the glass door. J-Dad served the guests things to drink, and they all talked and laughed a lot. When it got dark, L-Mom lit the candles on the tables.

After a long time, L-Mom announced the food was ready. Everyone went into the kitchen and took food back to their tables. They ate lots of stuff and listened to J-Dad's singing and his guitar noise. When the party was over, everyone left, and L-Mom snuffed out the pretty candles. I kept watching out the glass door, but my night vision eyes couldn't detect the disaster that was already happening. And then a horrible thing happened. L-Mom and J-Dad forgot about me, left me in solitary confinement, and went to bed!

'Help, someone help!" I called. "L-Mom, you forgot me." I called and called and finally got so tired, I collapsed on the floor and slipped into a long catnap.

G-Mom, *as I see it,* there was no reason why I could not have been out there. I would not only have been my friendly social self, I would have been on the lookout for any and all potential problems. I could have solved the disaster before it became a major catastrophe. The whole thing could have been prevented.

After what seemed like only a few minutes, I became aware of my super-danger whiskers trying to arouse me. I opened one sleepy eye and immediately knew the sun was thinking about making an appearance. The clue was a teeny tiny, tell-tail lessening of darkness in the morning sky. Hopefully my solitary confinement was nearly over, but I had not done any security patrolling. All my routines had crumbled!

L-Mom and J-Dad got up late, because I wasn't able to bang and bump on their door. I finally heard them rattling around in the kitchen.

"Help," I screamed. "Get me out of here!"

I kept making a terrible fuss until L-Mom finally opened the door. I raced to the open patio door and stared in amazement. And there it was; a total disaster of the first kind!

There were crumbs on the right, crumbs on the left, and into the messy patio marched the tiny 600. They marched so closely together they looked like single black lines. One line was marching in and another line was marching out with our crumbs. Apparently a scouting bug had smelled the dropped crumbs from the party and sneaked in through a crack under the screen door. He must have taken a sample back to his home and alerted the rest of his family. And there they were! Invaders! Hundreds of them! Acting as though they owned our crumbs!

I knew exactly what I had to do. I approached the two lines and demanded, "Who are you and who is in charge here?" No one answered. They were too busy marching and carrying.

I demanded again, "Hey, who are you and who is in charge? Who is the boss?"

One bug slowed down his marching and said, "We are scavenger sugar- ants."

"Aunts, are all of you aunts?"

"Yes," the bug answered.

"Aren't any of you uncles?"

No one answered me, so I decided to try my gentle approach. "Hey, you sugar- aunts, I'm in charge here. I have to keep order in this household. I do security patrolling every night looking for unwanted critters, and I am also a participating helper in all activities around here. I offer useful advice when needed. That is part of my job, *as I see it*. I also keep a vigilant lookout for all dangers. I have many rules, and one of them is to not allow bugs on the patio." I continued to explain, "In my unwanted absence last night, your whole army of sugar-aunts has marched in. So would you please kindly leave?"

Those busy sugar- aunts paid no attention to me so I put one paw on their lines and gently scattered a few of them to get their attention. Those silly sugar- aunts ran around in circles for a while but quickly returned to their marching lines. They continued to carry out crumbs and come back for more. I knew it would take them a whole month if I didn't get rid of them.

My antenna whiskers sensed their reluctance to leave and said to me, "Twitter, take action."

"Okay you sugar-aunts," I warned, "you will be sorry."

I took off and screamed, "L-Mom, where are you?"

I kept screaming and hunting until I found her in the laundry room. "L-Mom, there is a sugar-aunt army invasion on the patio! Come quickly! I asked them nicely, but they won't listen to me. They won't leave!"

L-Mom looked down at me and said, "Twitter, what is all the fuss? I'm really busy cleaning up things from last night's party."

I tried again to get her to come with me as I walked around and around and in between her legs. "I need help! There is a sugar-aunt army invasion on the patio. They keep marching in and out with our crumbs!"

"Twitter," she said, "I'll clean the patio in a little while."

Since L-Mom was busy, I went back out to check on the invasion.

"Oh no, this is terrible!" I shouted.

The sugar-aunt army had split. A flank off the incoming row had veered to the right. Apparently a scout had found a different kind of crumb and sent word back for more troops. Now I had an offshoot line of sugar-aunts under a patio chair. This new group was also marching back and forth to the crack like their comrades were doing. As I looked more closely, I realized, yet another group had found the mother lode of crumbs next to one of J-Dad's amplifiers.

This invasion problem needed to be solved, and I needed to make a plan. I decided to find L-Mom again while I was formulating a plan, but before my plan materialized, I saw L-Mom coming out on the patio with her vacuum cleaner.

Oh, no! I quickly realized what she was about to do. And she didn't have on her eye glasses. Perhaps her eyes were tired from taking care of the party guests and being up so late. Just as she bent down to plug in the vacuum cleaner, I raced over to stop her. I needed to get rid of the sugar-aunt army, but not *this* way.

"Stop," I screamed, "there are hundreds of sugar-aunts here. We need to make them go home!"

It was too late. L-Mom couldn't hear me because her noisy vacuum cleaner had roared to life.

"Go home!" I called to the sugar-aunts. "Go home quickly!"

L-Mom's vacuum cleaner roared back and forth as she swept the patio floor. It would soon be on the army lines, and L-Mom would not see them without her eye glasses. I stood close to the busy army and worried, as I watched them hurrying home with our crumbs. We didn't need the crumbs, and it was obvious L-Mom was trying to get rid of them.

My super-danger whiskers said to me, "Twitter, act quickly!"

Since the tiny sugar-aunts wouldn't listen to me, I put out one paw and gently scattered a few of them. They tumbled around and acted as silly as they had done the other time, but at least I got their attention.

"You have to go home!" I screamed. "L-Mom's vacuum cleaner will suck you up into the black bag, and you won't be able to get back to the uncles in your nest. Leave quickly!"

I guess my warning got to the boss aunt and she gave a signal to leave, because they immediately started scrambling for the crack. They didn't even stay in their straight lines anymore. I watched as the last one disappeared under the screen door's crack. I hoped they all got back home safely with the sugar-uncles.

Everything was pretty well back to normal by this evening. L-Mom popped corn for us, and we went into the family room to watch J-Dad's television station. I like to watch interesting programs. If a program is educational, I sit on the glass coffee table to be closer to the screen. If the program is about cooking, I pretend to watch as I take turns sitting on L-Mom and J-Dad's laps. I was just getting myself settled when one antenna whisker started to send alert signals. Pretty soon all my super-danger whiskers were telling me to be prepared-a major disaster was in the making!

G-Ma, I will contact you tomorrow night at midnight if I am still alive and well.

Love,
Twitter

CHAPTER 5

The Unwanted Gift

Dear G-Ma,

It was awful. It was worse than awful! It was like another midsummer nightmare. I thought the three of us were living a perfectly wonderful life! My scheduling was working fairly well and my security patrolling keeps our house perfectly safe. And now it looks as though my entire world might come to an end.

The biggest part of my day went along as usual. There were no disasters or anything suspicious. I had been on high alert, however, because my super-danger whiskers kept sending me signals. This high alert status was so stressful that I fell into a long, long, catnap in the late afternoon.

All of a sudden I was awakened by my whiskers. "Twitter, Twitter," they whispered to me, "you must wake up! You have missed everything!"

I sprang to my feet and looked around. My warm sunny spot on the carpet had moved clear across the room and was now half-way up the wall. It must have taken hours to do that.

"What time is it?" I shouted to myself?

Then I heard J-Dad in the music room making his guitar noise, and L-Mom in the kitchen rattling pots and pans. Again I shouted to no one, "When did they come home?"

My super-danger whiskers kicked in again with an urgent warning, so I raced to the kitchen. I needed to tell L-Mom about a coming danger so she could also be prepared.

As I rounded the hall corner to the kitchen, I nearly ran into something familiar. There stood my loathsome "go-to-the-vet" cat carrier! "What's going on here?" I shouted. "What is that thing doing here? It can't be time to go back to Dr. Gomley's office yet, because we were just there last week. Besides, all he wants to do is poke around all over me, and tell me to hold my breath while he takes pictures of my belly. That is pretty silly, *as I see it*. And he never hangs my belly pictures on his walls. Everyone hangs pictures of important people on their walls."

G-Ma, you know how I hate that cat carrier thing! It's like a dark cave. It feels as though I am in a prison. I can't move around in it, and my best catnip toy, Billy, doesn't get to go with me. Billy is even my best friend. And I can't get any little sips of water while I'm in there.

"L-Mom," I shouted again. "What is that dreadful 'go-to-the-vet' cat carrier doing here?"

L-Mom looked down at me and said, "I haven't had time to put it away yet."

"What did she mean by that?" I whispered aloud to myself, "I haven't gone anywhere in it." Her answer did not make any sense to me, and I needed to have an answer.

"What's going on?" I repeated as I walked in and out and between her legs.

"Twitter," she answered, "I'm fixing our dinner. Why don't you go and see what J-Dad is doing?"

L-Mom learned from me the way to keep things simple, so now she calls him J-Dad too. It is much simpler than calling him by his long name of Jack, *as I see it*.

Apparently L-Mom was too busy to tell me what was going on, and her request was strange because we could both hear J-Dad's guitar noise. We both already knew what he was doing. But, if she needed to know *exactly* what J-Dad was doing, I thought I had better find out and report back to her.

"J-Dad," I yelled as I raced to his music room, "what is going on? My dreaded 'go-to-the-vet' cat carrier is sitting in the hall, and L-Mom said she hadn't had time to put it away yet. I didn't go anywhere! Why is it sitting there?"

About that time, my super-danger whiskers were sending stronger signals.

J-Dad put his guitar down, and I jumped up on his lap. I put both front paws high on his chest and looked directly into his eyes.

"J-Dad," I said very seriously, "my whiskers are sending strong danger signals and I can't find out what is wrong. And, my dreaded 'go-to-the-vet' cat carrier is sitting in the hall. I just went to Dr. Gomley's office last week, and he did all the poking around stuff that he needed to do."

"Now Twitter, calm down," he said as he picked me up. He gave me his best loving kind of petting instead of his half-asleep television watching kind of petting. "Everything is going to be fine. Be patient. You will find out soon."

J-Dad seemed to be calm and not worried about whatever was going on, but my whiskers are never wrong. They were still warning me about some kind of trouble on its way.

After dinner we all went into the family room to watch television. Since I was still in high alert, I hoped an educational program would be on to distract me. I like to learn about things. My feline Mom told me all about animals, nature, and a lot of other stuff, but telling is not exactly believing, *as I see it"*

I jumped up on J-Dad's lap to get comfortable and immediately heard a strange sound. It seemed to be coming from the far end of the house. That sound did not belong there, so I got into my security mode, jumped to the floor, and cautiously crept down the hall to investigate.

As I got closer to the sound, it seemed to be an odd feline voice with a kind of twang. The bathroom door was shut, but the sound was definitely coming from behind the door. I quietly bent down to peek under it, but I couldn't see anything. I twisted my head in every direction, but my eyes couldn't get close enough to the floor. I then tried to slip one paw under the door, but there was not enough room to do that either.

"*Meeoowwwaa,*" something loudly and angrily roared inside the bathroom.

It didn't take me long to figure out it absolutely was a nasty feline voice with a Southern twang.

"Who's in there?" I demanded. I tried to make my voice sound authoritative, even though I was just a teeny bit frightened. I had never before heard an angry feline voice with a Southern twang. I remembered how my feline Mom always had such a sweet voice. As you know, that was a long time ago when I lived in the cozy cut-down cardboard box by the lady's back door. And my littermates, Gomer and

Harold, also had sweet little voices. The only other angry voice I ever heard was the humongous rat terrier dog: the one who chased me up the friendly tree. But his voice didn't have a Southern twang, or any other kind of twang.

Then the feline creature behind the bathroom door began scratching on it and continuing with more of its Southern twang howling. I figured out right away it was not going to answer me. L-Mom and J-Dad needed to know about this situation, so I raced back to the family room.

"L-Mom, J-Dad," I shouted, "come quickly! There is some kind of huge feline in the pool bathroom. It's making a lot of noise! It's scratching on the door and howling with a Southern twang!"

L-Mom looked at J-Dad and said, "I suppose we had better do it now. I really wanted to wait until tomorrow morning to give him a chance to settle in and get used to his new surroundings."

"Twitter," L-Mom said, "you stay right here. We will be back in a minute."

I didn't want to stay right there. I wanted to go with them. After all, I'm in charge of security and other stuff around here. *As I see it,* this qualified as a major security breach.

L-Mom and J-Dad went down the hall to the pool bathroom. I could hear them talking, but not clearly enough to know what they were saying. They stayed there and talked for a long time, and then they came back to the family room.

G-Ma, I wish you could have been here. You would not have believed your eyes! L-Mom was carrying a big white cat! She was petting it and talking sweetly to it.

"Twitter," L-Mom said, "we have a nice gift for you. Meet Alex. He used to live with Marianne. She is the lady from my office. She loves cats, but she said Alex just wasn't the right cat for her. She said he was very friendly and loving, but it was impossible for Alex to live with her any longer."

I wondered what Marianne meant by those strange statements.

L-Mom continued, "J-Dad and I thought he would be a good gift for you. Alex can keep you company when we are not here. That way you won't be lonely." With that, she put him down on the carpet about two yards in front of me.

My whiskers began sending stronger signals. They put me on my maximum alert status. I stood there, looked at that big cat, and whispered under my breath to myself, "Where did L-Mom and J-Dad get the idea I was lonely? Apparently they don't know, unlike dogs, cats did not evolve as pack animals. We don't need a bunch of animals like ourselves for protection or anything else. We can get along very well without another cat's help, and I don't need another cat to keep me company. I have all my good friends right here who keep me from getting lonely. Besides, I am too busy to be lonely. The last thing I need is another cat around here to disrupt my routines and security duties." They didn't hear me whispering, because I can whisper to myself without moving my lips.

Big Alex and I stood there staring at each other. Neither of us moved a muscle.

The most noticeable thing about Alex was his big size. He also had beautiful white fur and a long bushy tail. He continued to stare at me as he took a few large, elegant, commanding, sashaying steps toward me. Then he abruptly stopped. His steps were not at all like my nice little normal steps!

My whiskers told me an enormous problem had just developed. L-Mom and J-Dad wanted this big guy to join our household! I like to please them, so I needed to do some deep thinking about this new situation. I wished I had someone to help me figure out how to deal with it. I remembered a musical play I had seen on the television. There was a very troubled man named Tevye in the play, and he had a lot of problems. He was lucky, though, because he had a wise friend whose specialty was fiddling around on the roof. The little fiddler guy also gave Tevye good advice on how to solve all his problems. I wished we had a fiddler on our roof to give me advice, but we didn't have one.

Alex and I continued to stare at each other while I tried to figure out what advice the little fiddler guy would give to Tevye if Tevye had this problem. Then I could use his advice too. It didn't work, but suddenly something came to me in a flash! I could actually hear Tevye saying, "On the other hand, I have to make some sort of effort to welcome Alex. And on the other hand, he is definitely much bigger and more powerful than I am. And on the other hand, I need to find a way to maintain my position in this household. And on the other hand, I now have the mother of all problems, and it is named Alex."

G-Ma, I could hardly believe it! The little fiddler guy on the roof actually gave Tevye some wise advice, and Tevye passed it along to me. Tevye said it as if *he* had to deal with Alex instead of me. But the message was loud and clear. I wish I could thank the little fiddler on the roof for helping me.

Alex and I continued to stare at each other. My whiskers reminded me to be on guard and not show any sign of weakness, or I could lose my status and authoritative position around here. My whiskers were giving me the same advice as the little fiddler, so it had to be good advice. They also told me there can only be one queen bee in a bee's nest. Therefore, *as I see it,* Alex will have to know that I am the queen bee, and he is just a drone bee.

So I made a big decisive move. I said, "Hi." I tried to say it with great emphasis, but my greeting came out pitifully weak.

Alex didn't acknowledge my friendly greeting. He just sashayed a few more steps towards me.

As I looked very closely at his face, I couldn't believe my eyes! His face reminded me of the exact words my feline Mom said to me when we lived in the cozy cut-down cardboard box.

She had said, "Flitter, I want you to always remember something."

"Yes," I had said, "I will definitely remember something."

She then gave me more of her wise advice. "Always remember," she said, "to stick to the straight and narrow."

I didn't know what she meant at the time, but as I looked closely at Alex's face, her words became perfectly clear.

Among all his regular whiskers, Alex had one huge wide whisker. It certainly was not straight, and it definitely was not narrow. As far as sticking, it absolutely did! The last two inches at the end of the one wide whisker stuck straight up into the air! I ascertained, right then and there, that the up-bent whisker was, without a doubt, the sign of a big character flaw!

Another unusual feature on Alex's face was a little turned-up snarly area on the right side of his upper lip. It wasn't much, but I truly did detect it. His snarly upper lip was, without a doubt, another sign of a bad character flaw.

L-Mom had said Alex was a gift for me, but it wasn't my birthday or any other special day. One did not have to be a genius to figure out something was amiss. Then, like a flash, I remembered more of my

Mom's exact words. She had told me something about getting a gift, and a horse, and how I should never look in its mouth. I knew, from that moment on, I would stay far away from Alex's mouth.

G-Ma, that whole situation was beyond description. It was all so strange, and my whiskers were still sending danger signals. I could hardly wait until midnight to send you all these details. I need to take a tiny break now, go to the kitchen for a little sip of water, and do a short security patrol. Then I'll be right back to continue telling you about my first disturbing evening with Alex.

Love,
Twitter

CHAPTER 6

The Nasty Gift

Dear G-Ma,

Here I am again. All is secure, so I'll finish my e-mail. Alex continued to stare at me. His one wide whisker, with its end sticking straight up, wiggled in a very unfriendly way. I also noticed the small raised area on his upper lip began to go a wee bit higher as it turned into a big nasty looking sneer.

We stood there in the family room intently staring at each other. His sneer abruptly became more profound and menacing. He attempted to stare me down to gain the upper hand, but I calmly returned his gaze and flicked my tail as if to say, "I have the upper hand here by virtue of my seniority."

I knew it was important to have the upper hand, because a long time ago, my feline Mom told me something important. She said, "Flitter, I want you to always remember something." I said I would remember something, so she continued. "The upper hand that rocks the cradle is a good position to have." At least I think she said something close to that. I didn't know anything about rocking a cradle, but I knew I currently had the upper hand, and I needed to hang on to it to keep my position.

We continued to stare at each other while I contemplated the entire situation. *As I see it,* Alex certainly was not any kind of good gift for me. A good gift is a toy with some catnip in it, or a few pieces of Frisky Feline Fish Morsels all wrapped up in tissue paper with a red bow on the top. So if Alex was not really a gift what was he? Why was he here? Why couldn't he live with Marianne anymore? I concluded it was another mystery for me to solve. I thought we had all been getting along very nicely in this house. I dutifully did my security patrolling, toy delivering, awakening bedroom door bumps, and advice offerings. L-Mom was always busy doing her cooking, laundry, and go-to-the-office stuff. J-Dad did his pool cleaning, house chores, his guitar noise stuff, and driving up to fix the Fort Myers television station. I have a lot to do when they are here and when they are gone.

I didn't think I needed anyone to keep me company. I have a lot of company. My good friend, Shuggy, who lives across the street with Uncle Jerry and Aunt Vickie, comes over to our pool screen nearly every day. We have good conversations about his outdoor nighttime patrols and other important stuff. Our beautiful lime tree in the back yard is also a good friend of mine. It waves its pretty green leaves to me almost all day long. When I'm patrolling near it at the far corner of our pool screen, I wave my tail back and forth in answer. There are also a lot of birds that flutter in and out of its branches. The birds all chatter to me, because I don't think our lime tree has any kind of language to answer them back. And then there is my good friend the sun. I love the warm sunny spots on the carpet it gives me for my long catnaps.

The whole thing about Alex being a gift to me so I won't get lonely is very confusing. It is a big mystery, and there is something L-Mom and J-Dad are not telling me. This state of affairs reminded me of another thing my feline Mom told me to remember. It fits in precisely with this situation. I might have forgotten part of it, but I think she said, "There is something rotten in Detroit." Or maybe it was Denver. The thing I remember most about what she said, is that the city definitely started with the letter D. At any rate, I decided to keep my eyes and ears open until I figured out the mystery of Alex's arrival into our household, and the reason why he could not live with Marianne anymore.

After our long staring match, I decided I should be the first one to make an authoritative move. The move would have to be dynamic and set the tone for our co-existence. I stood a little taller, put my best paw forward and said, "C'mon, Alex, I'll show you around our house."

"So you are the leader and I am the follower? Are we going to play follow-the-leader?" he snarled, "and why are *you* the leader?"

As I headed toward L-Mom and J-Dad's bedroom, I thought about Alex's attitude. I looked around and saw him reluctantly doing his sashaying strut behind me. At that point, I knew I needed to reinforce my upper hand position.

"Part of my job," I said in my best formal grammar, "is to fiercely protect our house from the invasion of any and all unwanted critters and to diligently try to keep some sense of order. I don't allow anyone coming in here and willy-nilly upsetting the routine in this well-run household. It is plain to see that a routine and a well-run protected house is the best way to live, *as I see it*. I also give well thought out advice on anything and everything. Therefore, Alex, the bottom line is that I am the 'go-to-guy' around here." I was hoping my best formal grammar would help with this upper hand business.

Alex didn't seem to be interested, but I continued on anyway. I also needed to give him a little warning. "It may not be obvious, but I am able to do my security patrolling either awake or asleep. I can somehow, at any time, at the first sign of danger, be awakened instantly from a long catnap."

In no way was I going to tell Alex about my super-danger whiskers, because there was a huge chance he could be the cause of the danger signals I had been receiving. I definitely didn't want him messing around with my precious whiskers.

"I never heard of such a thing," he said, "why would anyone want to do all that work?"

"Alex," I said, "I don't consider it work. I think of it as an honor to have all this responsibility. L-Mom and J-Dad depend on me to hold up my end around here, and I intend to hold it up very high."

G-Ma, I hoped I had gotten the responsibility concept across to Alex so he could begin thinking about some productive roll he could play around here.

I turned to him when we reached the bedroom door and said, "Another thing I do during the night is deliver some of my toys right here for L-Mom. She likes to pick them up in the mornings and return them to my toy box."

"What toy box?" Alex snarled. I could see he was interested in my toy box.

"It's a cute little cut-down cardboard box in the family room," I answered.

"I had tons of toys when I lived at Marianne's place," he said with another snarl, "and they were all kept in a huge blue wicker basket."

"Why would anyone want tons of toys?" I asked.

"I wanted tons of toys so she got them for me. Marianne did everything I wanted her to do whenever I wanted her to do it. And that is all I'm going to say about that!"

The whole thing sounded like a convoluted conundrum to me. Marianne must have really liked Alex if she bought tons of toys for him, so why couldn't Alex live with her anymore? It definitely was a mystery to be solved. I decided to put it near the top of my to-do list.

We continued our tour to the kitchen. I showed Alex my food dish in the corner by the pantry.

"Where do I eat?' he abruptly asked.

I thought a lot about his question before I answered and decided to see if I could soften him up a bit. I finally said, "Well, you could share my dish."

"Then I would have to eat with you? I had my own private dish when I lived with Marianne, and it was a lot bigger than this one!"

I didn't have an answer for Alex, but I knew L-Mom would take care of it.

As we continued the tour of all the rooms inside and the pool patio outside, Alex's disparaging remarks about everything made my whiskers begin to send more warning signals. I knew right then and there, my new gift, in the form of Alex, was going to disrupt our household.

Our tour ended in the laundry room where I pointed out the big bathtub/laundry tub. "This is where L-Mom gives me a bath once in a while," I informed him.

Alex's eyes opened much wider, he arched his back and hissed, "What bath? I never had to take a bath, I don't want one, I am not going to have one, and I am not going to ever get wet!"

Well, G-Ma, that tirade was another shocker! I have to admit I am not a great proponent of baths, but L-Mom is so gentle and sweet when we do our bath thing. And she is careful to not get any soap in my eyes or ears. She dries me with a nice towel and talks to me the entire time. I actually prefer not to do the whole bath scene, but she convinced me a soapy bath was a good thing when she said, "Remember this Twitter, cleanliness is next to slipperiness." Or, it was something like that. I may not remember exactly what it is supposed to be next to, but L-Mom knows, and she will tell me if I really want to check on it.

"This bath business is one fight you are going to have to bring up with someone else, Alex," I quietly said as I left him staring at the bathtub/laundry tub.

I needed to do some deep thinking, so I went to hunt for my warm sunny spot on the family room carpet. I wish my sunny spot would stay in one place so it would be easier to find it, but it moves around all day.

"There you are!" I said as I walked into the room. But it wasn't big enough anymore. There was only a tiny bit hiding under the glass table that holds all of L-Mom's valuable seashells.

I immediately went to plan B: the washing machine. I jumped up on it because I needed to be alone, and I like to be up high so I can see all around me. I allowed my eyes to go shut after a short time because I can do deep thinking much better that way.

My thinking, however, was soon interrupted by Alex's loud voice.

"Hey," he demanded as he jumped up beside me. "I want to talk to you."

I opened one eye to peek at him and saw that wide up-bent whisker waving in the air.

"Okay Alex, what is it?"

"Why did you have to come here to live? What's wrong with *you*?"

Did he think something was wrong with me? Perhaps my life's history from the cozy cut-down cardboard box to the rescue in the woods and continuing with my adoption, would explain my position in this household. And it might be the first step toward changing his bad character flaw.

"Sit down here beside me Alex. I want to explain some things to you" I said.

Alex sat down and listened. I finished my history by telling him how I explored this wonderful house, how lucky I felt to be rescued, and that the best part was becoming an adoptee.

Alex stared at me with a menacing look in his eyes. That one up-bent whisker began to wiggle. His upper lip curled into his trademark sneer, and he said, "I don't believe a word of it. Whoever heard of an adoptee? It is too far-fetched. Marianne purchased me at a prestigious cat show. My Mother was entered in a competition, and she won the first prize. Therefore, I am very pedigreed."

Alex was acting in a very arrogant manner, and it didn't make much sense to me that he would admit to such a bad thing as being pedigreed. It sounded like some horrible feline disease. Or, maybe the "ped" part of it referred to a paw deformity that I had overlooked. Not wanting to embarrass him about it, I thought I would think it over for a while. Perhaps I could figure it out later. Then Alex jumped down and sashayed toward the kitchen.

I tried to resume my thinking mode, but all at once my super-danger whiskers alerted me. I slightly opened one eye and saw Alex coming back toward me with his head down, his lip making that snarl look, and his up-bent whisker wiggling in the air. All those signs told me to be ready for trouble.

He jumped up on the washing machine again and snarled to me, "There is no such thing as an adoptee!"

I stared at him as he jumped back down and left me alone. I needed to be alone to do some more deep thinking about all these new developments. After a long while, I went into the family room. L-Mom and J-Dad had gone to bed and had not even said goodnight to me. They always petted me, told me to have a good night, and to keep up my excellent patrolling. All of a sudden I felt lonely and sad. And then I saw the most disturbing thing of all: Alex was asleep in *my* toy box!

I think my blood sugar must have been low because I started to cry. But then I figured out the strain of Alex's arrival was too much for L-Mom and J-Dad, and that was the reason they forgot about me.

My whiskers kept sending me more danger signals as I patrolled. I searched diligently all around the house, but all seemed to be in order. I got thirsty so I went to get a little sip of water. I put my head down, stuck out my tongue, and there he was! He was swimming in my drinking water!

"Who are you?" I demanded.

"I'm Freddie-the-fruit-fly," he answered weakly.

"What are you doing in my drinking water?" I asked.

He looked up at me but didn't answer, so I asked, "Why are you swimming in my water dish?"

The little guy kept swimming in my drinking water. First he swam forward doing the breaststroke, and then he did the backstroke. He kept going around and around and making little waves.

At exactly that moment I remembered back to our cozy cut-down cardboard box and my Mom saying to me, "Flitter, always remember this. Don't make any waves!" I didn't understand what she meant, because I had no plans to ever go swimming or get wet.

"You have to stop swimming around in there right now," I said. "I have routines and rules, and I can't have anyone making waves. How did you get in here?' I added.

He kept swimming and making waves. Finally he looked up at me and breathlessly said, "Yesterday I flew in through one of the tiny holes in the pool screen."

"Well what are you doing in my water dish?' I asked again.

"I don't really want to be in here. I am so tired! I have been trying to get out, but every time I get close to the sides of your swimming pool my feet slip. The sides are too wet, and too high, and too slippery," he explained.

"In the first place," I informed him in my most authoritative voice, "it is not my swimming pool. It's my drinking water. In the second place, the only time I swim is when I accidentally fall into the real swimming pool. And in the third place, what are you doing in the house in the first place?"

"I was only looking for some fruit. I eat fruit. After all, that is why I am called a fruit fly. I thought I smelled some fruit while flying around outside in your yard," he answered.

"Well, we had some grapes earlier tonight, but L-Mom and J-Dad ate them all," I said.

Freddy-the-fruit-fly looked up at me with his sad, teeny tiny black eyes and pleaded, "Will you help me out of here? I didn't drink any of your swimming pool water or do anything else in it."

I could tell right then and there little Freddie-the-fruit-fly was in deep trouble and didn't comprehend much of what I had told him, so I gently put one paw into my drinking water and got it under him. I put him on the floor and said, "I want you to listen carefully. If I dry you off, will you fly over to the sliding glass door that leads out to the pool screen and wait there until morning? J-Dad opens that door as soon as he gets up. Then you can fly out through any screen hole you want. After that, you can look for fruit somewhere else. Try looking under our lime tree. Will you do that?"

I knew those directions were probably way over his head, but I cannot talk in simple terms. My brain does not work that way. Besides, since he was so tiny, he probably had a very small brain.

"Okay," he said.

I blew my warm breath on his tiny wings until they were dry. "Can you fly now?" I asked.

"Yep," he said as he circuitously flew toward the sliding glass door. I knew he flew in circles trying to get to the door, because his radar was still a little damp, and therefore, he couldn't fly in a straight line.

Well, G-Ma, I have had an exhausting day and an interesting night so far. And it is only midnight! I'll continue to look after Freddie-the-fruit-fly until morning and report it all to you tomorrow night. I'm sure the Alex problem will keep my super-danger whiskers alert until I get it solved.

Love,
Twitter

CHAPTER 7

The Invention

Dear G-Ma,

I kept my eyes on Freddie-the-fruit-fly all night while continuing my security patrolling. I was really thirsty for a little sip of water, but to be on the safe side, I thought it best to wait until L-Mom washed my dish and put in fresh water. Little Freddie-the-fruit-fly stayed on the sliding glass door the rest of the night. When J-Dad opened the door in the morning, my new little friend flew out as promised. I think he even made a little wave to me with one wing. He certainly liked to make waves. I learned at that moment there was more than one kind of wave.

Our morning progressed as usual, so I thought everything was going along swimmingly. Swimmingly is a new word I just added to my vocabulary. I invented it after my experience with Freddie-the-fruit-fly. I am trying very hard to improve my education. Since it was Saturday, L-Mom was flying around doing her laundry and week-end chores, and J-Dad puttered around cleaning the pool before going into his music room to do his guitar noise stuff.

"J-Dad!" I shouted as I trotted behind him into his music room. "Do you need me for anything?"

J-Dad looked down at me with a smile on his face and said, "Not right now, Twitter. Why don't you go somewhere all by yourself and have a nice extra-long catnap?"

I had been very busy during the night and helped both of them with everything this morning, so the thought of a long catnap never occurred to me. It sounded like a great idea. I raced into the family room to see where my good friend, the sun, had put my nice warm sunny spot on the carpet. For some reason, the sun moves it to different places all the time.

"There you are!" I said as I found it next to the television. I got on it and squirmed all around. Then I rolled over onto my stomach and stretched my front paws out as far as possible. I slowly raised my hips as high as they would go. I kept that pose for a long time because it is one of my favorites. Then I rolled over onto my back and put all four paws in the air. I tried very hard to go to sleep, but my mind would not rest. It was too busy thinking about the super-special thing I had been thinking about for a long time. It told me the time had come to put all its thinking into action. But first I needed a little sip of water. As I was headed back to my warm sunny spot, I turned the corner, and there, guarding the doorway, was Alex!

He stood stiffly as he blocked the door opening and glared at me with a decidedly defiant look. The curl on his upper lip rose higher. There was barely enough room for me to get past him if I continued on, but to do that would be to concede defeat and allow Alex to have the upper hand. I definitely could not let that happen, because if he had the upper hand, it would be a disaster of the first class.

"Where are you going?" he snarled at me as I stood in front of him.

"I'm going back to my warm sunny spot and start working on my invention," I defiantly answered as I drew myself up a little taller.

Ole Alex cocked his head to one side and looked questioningly at me. I'm calling him "Ole Alex" now because of his attitude and character flaw. But I won't call him that out loud. At that moment a memory came to me in a flash! I remembered again one of the important things my Mom told me when we lived in our cozy cut-down cardboard box by the lady's back door. She said, "Flitter, I want you to always remember something." I said I would always remember something, so she continued. "Always remember that curiosity killed the cat." The meaning of her words also came with the flash, and now I knew I had Ole Alex right where he needed to be. Ole Alex was curious! There was no way I was going to kill Ole Alex, but I absolutely knew at that moment his curiosity resulted in the upper hand remaining with me.

He cocked his head even more and asked, "What invention?"

In order for my words to have the best effect, I spoke very slowly and emphasized every word. "It is a program soon to be known as *Animal's Aerobic Alphabetic Actions,* and commonly to be called *Twitter's Triple A.* I know the title has four 'A's, and its common name of *Twitter's Triple A* has only three 'A's in it, but it has to be that way, because everyone knows the words, 'Triple A,' but whoever heard of 'Quadruple A'? Anyway, it is an important two part program. My invention is specifically designed to be educational by teaching the alphabet along with the use of healthy aerobic poses and actions."

Alex kept his head cocked and said, "That sounds pretty fishy. Whoever heard of an aerobic alphabet?"

Trying to maintain the upper hand, again I answered very slowly while emphasizing every word. "No one has ever heard of it. That is why I am inventing it!"

Alex cocked his head a little more as he tried to comprehend the very easy explanation I had just given him. He finally asked, "What good is it?"

It was evident Ole Alex was getting curiouser and curiouser. I had one more card to play in this "poker hand," so I metaphorically put it on the table and said, "Step aside, Alex, and I will demonstrate."

G-Ma, as you can see, I am adding new big and important words to my growing vocabulary.

Ole Alex then stepped aside, and I slowly walked through the doorway past him, instantly knowing the upper hand was back in my court. Or that something like that had just happened.

I stepped sprightly as I led the way into the family room and looked around for my warm sunny spot. "There you are!" I said when I found it. My spot was in front of J-Dad's lounge chair and seemed to be trying to crawl under the chair and hide from me again. I plopped down and wiggled around on my spot to do some warm-ups before getting into the first position. I held the position while looking up at Ole Alex to see his reaction.

"What is that suppose to be?" he asked.

"This is the first action of the program. It is obviously and understandably called the 'A-B-C Position,' which is short for 'Aerobic Back C.' One's getting into, and then holding the position is a big important part of the program." I explained it as simply as possible.

"I don't get it," Alex grumbled.

"Okay Alex," I said slowly, "let me demonstrate it again from the very beginning." I righted myself, took a couple of deep breaths, plopped back down on the carpet, and wiggled all around. "One must always do warm-ups," I instructed. I continued to demonstrate as I gave very clear explanations in my best formal grammar. "One turns on one's right side. Then one slowly stretches one's front paws high over the head, extending the back legs out also, as far as possible, and curls backward into an elongated, curvy letter C. Then one holds the pose for a nice long period of time."

"What good is it?" he snarled.

I was beginning to loose patience with Alex, but since he needed to understand these simple concepts, I decided to keep trying. Again, I slowly said, "Alex, I have a very logical mind and this position is the beginning of the alphabet. Learning and doing the positions and actions will help to keep you limber and healthy. You can also meditate while holding the positions. You can think about your problems and possibly find solutions to them. It is even possible to have a change of attitude about a lot of things while meditating." I slipped that little suggestion in on the chance Ole Alex might take the hint. "It also is educational. Everyone should start a formal education by learning the alphabet. When I finish inventing the program, the entire animal population, and especially the feline contingent, will not only be healthier, they will be better educated."

I then uncurled my back, returned my feet to their normal position and looked up at him. He still seemed attentive so I proceeded on to the next aerobic action position of "*Twitter's Triple A.*"

"As we move on through the alphabet," I explained, "we come to the next action named the 'D-E-F Position,' which is short for 'Dancing Energized Feet.' As it implies, the purpose is to create energy in your feet, which then continues to your entire body. I shall now demonstrate and repeat the exact words as they will be written in the instructional manual."

"One begins by standing straight and erect while taking four deep breaths. This will get you into a meditative frame of mind. Next, one extends the right front foot forward while saying, 'you put the right foot in.' The action continues as you return the right foot to its starting position and swing it behind you while saying, 'you put the right foot out.' Continue the action by repeating the aforementioned first action of putting the right foot forward, again saying, 'you put the right foot in,' and adding, 'and you shake it all about.' This is a prolonged shaking action by the right foot."

I took a deep breath and continued with the program's instructions and my demonstration. "You have now fulfilled the 1st part of the 'Dancing Energized Feet Position.' The exact same dancing movement is then repeated with the left front foot. In the concluding segment of this position, you say, 'and you turn yourself around.' This final action is accompanied with high stepped dancing movements done in a complete circle."

I looked at Alex and said, "As you can see, Alex, it is all very simple and well described. Anyone would be able to understand it. All you have to do is put your mind to it."

Alex shook his head and walked away with his up-bent whisker waving to no one. *As I see it,* Ole Alex was definitely impressed.

I relaxed the 'D-E-F Position' and stretched out on the warm sunny spot. I needed to rest a bit before working some more on my *Twitter's Triple A* invention. I also wanted to think of ways to change Alex's character flaw. Then some words came to me from when we were in our cozy cut-down cardboard box. Mom had warned me about trying to change things. She had said something about not being able to change a silk purse into something else, but I can't remember her exact words. I don't have a silk purse, so maybe it is all right to try to change his character flaw.

Well, G-Ma, we all got through the rest of day without a major disaster, but my super-danger whiskers keep warning me about more big trouble headed my way. Nothing unusual happened during my security patrolling tonight. The silly clock in the kitchen, with its fake bird sounds, told me it was midnight, so I rushed to our computer to send the daily news to that place where you live. I know how important it is for you to hear about your family. I'll contact you again tomorrow night at midnight. Perhaps my super-danger whiskers are wrong, but with Alex here now, it is unlikely.

Love,
Twitter

CHAPTER 8

The Watering Pail

Dear G-Ma,

My super-danger whiskers kept alerting me the rest of the night to some kind of trouble coming my way, and Shuggy did a lot of unusual barking all night. I rushed to the living room each time he barked so I could jump up on the lamp table to see what going on, but all I could see was Shuggy running around and around Uncle Jerry and Aunt Vickie's house. I hope he caught whatever he was chasing. Sometimes he chases his tail around and around, but last night it was an entire house.

I delivered some toys to L-Mom and J-Dad's bedroom door at the scheduled time. Billy, my favorite catnip toy mouse, wanted to be delivered, so I put him over by the side of their door so he wouldn't get stepped on. And I bumped on their door at the usual time even though it was Sunday morning. I know they don't get up as early on the weekends, but I like to keep to my routines. Life is simpler that way, *as I see it.*

They finally got up and did the usual puttering around in the kitchen. L-Mom put our breakfast in our two dishes and gave us our special weekend piece of *Frisky Feline Fish Morsels.* She only gave us one pathetic little piece though. That is all we ever get, but I always hope she will forget and give us another one. She is always worried about everyone's diets. Maybe I would grow as big as Alex if I had all I wanted. I love those little things!

It had been a long and troubling night, so I decided a nice morning catnap was in order. I went into the family room to look for my warm sunny spot on the carpet. "There you are!" I said as I spotted it on the far wall near my scratching post. It was still tiny this early in the morning, so I had to curl up into a tight ball to fit on it. My eyes had barely closed when my super-danger whiskers alerted me again. I slightly opened one eye and saw Ole Alex coming. His head was down, his lip was making that snarl look, and his up-bent whisker was wiggling in the air. All those signs told me to be ready for trouble.

I peeked out of one eye as Ole Alex began circling me. "Fffftt, fffftt, fffftt," he spat at me, "you are a freaky feral feline!"

I opened both eyes in amazement and sprang to my feet.

"What did you say?" I indignantly asked.

"Fffftt, fffftt, fffftt. You are a freaky feral feline!" he spit out again.

Alex continued to circle me and spit those horrible untrue words at me.

"Hold on, Alex," I said as I tried to calm down both of us, "you are too upset and entirely wrong. You need to take a few deep breaths and have a nice long catnap."

He stopped circling me and snarled, "There is no such thing as a *long* catnap, and *you* are a freaky feral feline."

"I am an adoptee!" I shouted to him as I ran to find L-Mom. I desperately needed some guidance.

"L-Mom," I screamed as I ran to the kitchen. "I need help! Alex is calling me a freaky feral feline and spitting at me. I'm sure he has his whiskers crossed or something. I need your help right now!"

L-Mom looked down at me and smiled as she said, "Twitter, calm down. You are imagining things again and making much ado about nothing. I'm sure Alex is saying 'furry family friend.' He is probably trying to be friendly."

"I am not imagining things, and I am not making too much ado about nothing," I protested. "He called me bad names. And that is the absolute truth, *as I see it.*"

L-Mom continued to busy herself with kitchen work, so I dejectedly walked to the laundry room where I could be alone. I kept thinking about everything on the way. I was pretty sure L-Mom knew exactly what Alex was calling me. Perhaps she was protecting him until she could have one of her heart-to-heart talks with him. We have those talks when she thinks I get something a little mixed up. Usually it is only a tiny thing I have mixed up and is hardly worth all the bother.

I then went back to the family room and saw Ole Alex sashaying toward the patio as if he owned the entire house. It was obvious he was thinking about getting into some mischief out there. The prudent thing for me to do, therefore, was to keep my eye on him.

Our Florida summer had once again brought us its daily heavy wash of rain. My paws got dampened as I stepped through the sliding glass doors, and my nose was filled with the rain's legacy of clean refreshing smells. A few deep breaths revitalized me as I went in search of Ole Alex.

I turned right and started to walk past one of L-Mom's huge, bushy, potted plants. There was a big plastic watering pail sitting on the deck beneath its leaves. I was nearly past the watering pail when all of a sudden I thought my right eye caught some movement on the top of the pail. I knew in that instant it had to be one of those sneaky little green lizards!

Something needed to be done before that little guy slipped into the house through the open glass doors. I looked up at the top of the pail but could not see him. The pail was way too tall. I then went around to the back of the pail and looked up.

"Where is he?" I whispered to myself. "That little guy is up there somewhere." I couldn't see him or reach him, even when I stretched up on my hind legs. This was a major disaster in the making! What was I to do? Ole Alex's mischief would have to wait, because stray sneaky lizards are a top security breach. I needed to get higher to search for that pesky little guy.

My whiskers began telling me, "Think Twitter, think!"

The answer came to me in a flash. I heard a little voice in my head say, "Crouch down, jump high, get a good hold on the rim of the plastic watering pail, and then pull yourself up the rest of the way!"

It seemed like an excellent plan, but something was holding me back. I stood there staring at the tall pail and continued to think about the flash that had just brought me its answer. All of a sudden I remembered my Mom's words of advice. "Flitter, he who hesitates is lost."

That did it! With Mom's words ringing in my ears, I instantly gave a mighty leap toward the rim of the watering pail. While in midair, I had a prophetic suspicion that the plan was faulty for some reason. And then I remembered the rest of Mom's advice. "Flitter, always look before you leap!" But it was too late at that point to heed the rest of

Mom's advice. I grabbed the rim of the pail with both front paws, but my weight pulled it over, and its contents nearly drowned me!

Splash! Evidently the pail was full of water! How was I supposed to know that? I stood there in a big wet puddle! I was drenched with water! It was in my eyes and ears! And to add to my problems, the sneaky little green lizard had gotten away.

I ran into the house to search for J-Dad while dripping water all over L-Mom's nice clean floors.

"J-Dad" I shouted, "I need you! Where are you?"

I ran to his music room but he wasn't there. Then I heard a familiar sound coming from his bathroom. I ran in that direction still dripping water all over the carpet and tile floors along the way. J-Dad was standing in front of his mirror. He was using the noisy gadget that takes all the fur off his face.

I screamed loudly so he could hear me over his face-fur gadget. "J-Dad, help! A terrible thing has happened! I am all wet, there is water in my eyes and ears, the watering pail is upset, and the sneaky little green lizard got away."

J-Dad unplugged the face-fur gadget and looked down at me. He started to laugh, but I knew he realized the seriousness of the situation. Even with water in my ears, I clearly heard him say, "Twitter, you certainly are a sight with sore eyes."

My eyes were not sore. They were just full of water. J-Dad must have thought they were sore though. He is really smart about things like that. I could tell by his laughing voice that he was feeling sorry for me. He picked me up and got a big towel to wrap around me. Then he carried me to his lounge chair in the family room.

"Twitter," he said as he sat down, "let's sit here a little bit until you get dry, and you can tell me what you were doing with the watering pail."

J-Dad wiped me all over with the nice big towel. He also gave me a lot of good petting in between towel wipes. I began to feel a lot better after getting dry and relating all the patio details.

"What happened to the lizard?" J-Dad asked, "are you sure there really was one?"

"Well, the fleeting glance I got of it certainly looked like a lizard to me," I answered, "he was the same color as L-Mom's huge, bushy, potted plant that was sitting right beside it. The sneaky little green guy probably jumped over into the plant when the pail tipped over on me, and he is now hiding in the plant leaves. I definitely know he is going to create a problem for my security patrolling. And that is a major security breach, *as I see it*."

J-Dad petted me under my chin and said, "Twitter, you are dry now, so I am going to go to the music room. Why don't you take one of your long catnaps and relax for a while?"

"Okay," I answered, "but first I need to work on my invention."

"What are you inventing?" J-Dad asked.

"It is a marvelous invention titled, *Animal's Aerobic Alphabetic Actions*. But *Twitter's Triple A* is what it will commonly be called. It is an exercise program designed to be educational, because it teaches the alphabet through the use of aerobic poses and actions."

G-Ma, I had to spend a lot of time memorizing the introduction and the formal directions to my invention, because it is a bit confusing.

I eagerly said to J-Dad, "Would you like a demonstration?"

J-Dad hesitated a little and finally asked, "Will it take long?"

"No, no," I quickly answered, "I am still at the beginning of the alphabet, so I will only explain and demonstrate the 'G-H-I' position. That is short for 'Getting Hips Inclined.'"

I jumped down to find my warm sunny spot on the carpet. "There you are!" I said as I found it in front of our television set. I took four deep breaths, plopped down on my spot, and wiggled all around.

"Those were just the warm-ups," I explained, "I shall now give you the formal directions as they will be written in the instructional manual."

"One gets on one's belly and extends one's front paws straight ahead as far as possible. Then one slowly begins to raise one's hips as high as possible. When one gets as high as one can go, one has one's hips in an inclined position, thereby fulfilling the entire 'G-H-I' parts of the title. One holds this position for a good long time. The extension of the front paws, the raising of the hips as far as possible, and the holding of oneself in this inclined position, results in a stretching of all relevant muscles." I righted myself once again and looked up at J-Dad for his reaction.

J-Dad gave me an approving smile as he headed toward his music room and said, "Twitter, you are really something. But I just don't know what." And with that endorsement, J-Dad headed for his music room.

Those nice words made me smile too. Then I said to my warm sunny spot, "Now don't move too far away, because I am going to take a nice long catnap on top of you."

I stretched my body to its fullest and twisted and contorted in a lot of different positions. I tried relaxing on my tummy, on my back with both feet in the air, and even with my head turned up to the ceiling. Finally I just curled up into a ball and closed my eyes.

I drifted off for a long catnap, but it didn't happen. My whiskers sent me a danger signal, and I felt the presence of Alex. A little peek with one eye revealed Ole Alex sashaying and strutting up to me. He gave me his sly conniving look and said, "Hee, hee, hee. I know something you don't know. And you are in deep, deep trouble."

Well, G-ma, he certainly put an end to my catnap. Right now I have to get a little sip of water, look on the kitchen floor for a dropped Frisky Feline Fish Morsel, and do a security check. Then I'll tell you the deep trouble Ole Alex gleefully revealed to me.

Love,
Twitter

CHAPTER 9

The Security Breach

Dear G-Ma,

My security patrolling didn't take long, so I'm back here at our computer to finish telling you what nearly gave me nineteen nervous breakdowns.

Ole Alex's taunt really got my attention. "What deep, deep trouble?" I demanded as I sprang to my feet from my warm sunny spot on the family room carpet. Obviously something was not right in our house. Shifty Ole Alex knew about it and was now blaming me. My first suspicion was that Ole Alex caused whatever was wrong, and he wanted me to get blamed for it. This suspicion is based on my accurate supposition that he has a history of mischief; a history rich and varied. I am sure it dates back to his Marianne-living days. Or possibly to the up-bent whisker which obviously signifies a character flaw.

"What is going on and why am I going to be in deep, deep trouble?" I repeated.

Ole Alex looked at me with hooded eyes and slyly smiled. He was definitely attempting to get the upper hand again. I thought we had settled that issue some time ago. Apparently Alex needed a little review and it could not wait.

"Alex," I calmly said, "I am the Alpha Male around here. Besides, I have seniority." I didn't want to bring up the absolute fact about me being an adoptee, which is a pretty highly placed position in the social world, *as I see it*. To bring it up would not have been kind. After all, it was not Alex's fault that he couldn't win any prizes when he went to all those cat shows with his mother.

"As you know," I calmly continued so as not to appear duly alarmed, "it is my job to do security patrolling around here so everyone, including you, is kept safe and sound. And, I also try to keep order and some sense of routine. I have found life is so much simpler when everyone keeps to a regular routine. Now if something is wrong, you must inform me immediately." It seemed to me this review was quite adequate, so I turned my attention back to the little game of one-upmanship he was playing with me.

"Now let's get on with this current situation and get it resolved," I said. I knew something was amiss and I desperately needed to get to the bottom of it, but I didn't dare allow him to see how concerned I was. He was enjoying my dilemma and his little game too much. Alex had something I wanted. Knowledge! So I needed to go along with his game and play my cards close to my chest!

"Alex," I went on, "We have a situation here and it needs to be resolved. L-Mom and J-Dad do not want anything to get out of control. Now, one of us must handle it. If you caused it, I suggest you remedy it, and if you did not cause it, whatever it is, I will have to fix it. Now, you either take care of it, or tell me what it is so the problem can properly be disposed of immediately."

I was bragging just a little bit about my ability to take care of whatever it was, but I needed to call Ole Alex's bluff. He pretends he never sees any of the problems around here when, in fact, he causes most of them. Then, the solution usually requires my expertise.

Ole Alex's upper lip rose slowly and turned into a nasty sneer. He finally said, "The little green lizard from the patio sneaked in here while you were gyrating, and inventing, and sleeping on your warm sunny spot. If you had been vigilant, which is your job, you would have seen it."

With the news of a sneaky little green lizard in the house, I dropped my bluffing game and concentrated on my security duties. After all, my reputation was at stake!

"What little green lizard? I don't even allow lizards on the patio! How could one be in here? Where is he now?"

Ole Alex put a bigger sneer on his face and said, "It is the same little green lizard from the watering pail. When you upset it on yourself, and nearly drowned yourself, and looked totally silly, he jumped into the leaves of the tall potted plant. I saw the whole thing."

"Where is he now?" I screamed, "I have to get him out of here! Where is he?"

"I'm not telling. It's none of my business. It is supposed to be your business. I'm on my way to get a drink of water.

With that, Ole Alex sashayed off toward the kitchen, and I'm afraid he took the upper hand with him.

I raced after Alex and shouted, "Alex, where is the sneaky little green lizard? How did he get in here?"

Alex didn't stop. He didn't turn around. He didn't answer. He proceeded onward, picking his legs up high with each step as though strutting down a football field with the entire opposition far behind, proudly carrying the ball for the victorious touchdown. In reality, I feared, he could figuratively be carrying our upper hand. When he reached our water bowl, he leaned down and took only one tiny sip. It was obvious he didn't really need or want a drink of water. He was just playing his game of "one-upmanship by getting Twitter's goat."

"Alex," I finally pleaded, "time is passing away. You must tell me. Stop fooling around."

Alex slowly turned and looked at me. It was more than obvious he was toying with me and enjoying every minute of it. His eyes were hooded again and his upper lip had its familiar sneer shape. "Okay," he said, "he sneaked in through the open sliding glass door."

"You already told me that. Stop waving your up-bent whisker and tell me more. What did he do? Where did he go? Where is he now? Answer quickly! Hurry!"

I was getting frantic. A sneaky little green lizard inside the house was unacceptable! It was totally against my rules. My reputation was at stake. This security breach had to be dealt with swiftly and successfully. But first I needed to find the sneaky little green guy.

"Well," Alex continued, "he crept in on the carpet, looked around, saw you cat napping, and took a few hesitating steps."

With that, Ole Alex started to walk way, again doing his arrogant strutting steps.

"Alex, what happened to him then? Where is he?"

Alex stopped and turned around to give me a sly look and said, "He scooted across the family room floor and went into the bathroom; the one next to the music room. I followed him to ask if he also got soaked with the watering pail water. The same water you spilled all over yourself. But he was too fast for me. That little guy could really move. He slid right under the linen closet door and disappeared."

With the news of the sneaky little green lizard's location, I ran to the bathroom and stood in front of the linen closet's doors. As you know, G-Ma, the linen closet has those two bi-fold doors that are hinged in the center. I know all about doors because I'm almost certain I remembered my Mom saying, "Flitter, there are doors out in the big world called 'bi-fold.' The word 'bi' means two, therefore, there are two separate doors and they are held together in the center. They operate the way pages of a book open and close. There is a big difference though. All books open by having their spine away from you. The spine acts like a hinge. Bi-fold doors open the opposite way. Their spine comes toward you as you open them. The best way to remember it is to think of bi-fold doors as backwards books."

Way back there in our little cozy cut-down cardboard box, I didn't know what a book or a door was, but I tried to remember everything my Mom told me. Once I became an "adoptee," and came to live here with L-Mom and J-Dad, I learned all about books and doors, and it is pretty important stuff to know.

I knew the little guy was behind those doors, because I can sense lizards with my antenna whiskers. Besides, Ole Alex told me he was in there. The first thing I did was put one paw under one of the bi-folds, remembering that it was designed after a backwards book, and tried to pull it forward. The door rattled and rattled as I tried to open it. Nothing was working so I stuck my other paw under the door and wiggled it all around. My only reward was more rattling. I pulled my paw back and put my head down to the crack at the bottom to see if I could see the little guy. It was too dark to see anything and there was nothing I could do if I did see him.

"Hey, you in there," I called, "come out right now! You can't be in the house!"

He didn't answer me. I didn't think he would, but it was worth a try.

I then got on my side and slipped my paw under the hinge between the doors. Perhaps, if I got a good hold under there, the door might move forward enough for me to slip in.

"Twitter, what in the world are you doing?" J-Dad called to me from his computer room.

J-Dad instinctively knew I was the one making the noise. He knows how hard I try to keep everything under control around here, and with all the noise, he knew there was some kind of problem. He also knew I was attempting to solve it.

I was terribly frantic at that point. My head wouldn't fit under the door, my paws wouldn't open the doors, and I couldn't reach in far enough to get the lizard.

I didn't answer J-Dad because I was too busy. I kept right on pawing and rattling those doors until J-Dad came into the bathroom.

"What in the world is going on?" he said as he came up to me.

I ignored him and kept up with my frantic pawing and rattling.

And then it happened! J-Dad opened that backwards book, bi-fold door, and the sneaky little green lizard scampered out, ran straight through J-Dad's legs, and escaped into the family room before I could get around J-Dad's legs.

I skidded around on the tile floor and finally passed J-Dad as we all ran into the family room. Ole Alex was sitting by the open patio door watching us, so I knew the sneaky little green lizard had not gone outside. He was still in the family room somewhere.

"Where is he, Alex?" I screamed. "Where did he go?"

Ole Alex waved his up-bent whisker at me as he walked away and said, "It is none of my business."

Well, G-Ma, the rest of my afternoon and evening was totally ruined. No one helped me look for the sneaky little green lizard. No one seems too worried about the pesky little guy. I was a nervous wreck. After all, it was a huge security breach. Tomorrow I am going to formulate a fool proof plan to find him. I know I can do it! Wish me luck.

Love,
Twitter

CHAPTER 10

The Lizard's Tale

Dear G-Ma,

This morning I helped L-Mom and J-Dad get started on things they had planned for today. It was good that they didn't need me for much, because I had a huge problem with the missing little green lizard. I started my search by walking all around the perimeter of the family room. Nothing! The little guy was hiding very well from me and undoubtedly watching and laughing at me.

As I pondered the situation, my trusty whiskers said to me, "Twitter, the first thing to do is to make a foolproof plan. Think long and hard, and plan it well."

That was good advice, so I looked around for my warm sunny spot on the carpet. "There you are!" I said as I saw it hiding half under the couch. I curled up on it and thought and planned. Soon I was able to formulate a stupendous foolproof plan. Truthfully, I sort of stole the sneaky little green lizard's plan: since he was hiding from me, I would hide from him. Then, when he got tired of hiding and decided to leave, I would jump out and capture him. It was a fantastic foolproof plan.

I squeezed behind the couch and waited for him to show himself. And I waited. And I waited. By afternoon I was really getting discouraged. Perhaps I hadn't thought long or hard enough while making my plan. Perhaps my plan was working, but the truth of it had not yet materialized. Perhaps it needed a slight revision. "Yes," I whispered to myself, "a revision is in order. Perhaps he saw my hiding place. I am now going to move from one hiding place to another."

I then crawled behind the television set. And I watched for just a short time. Then I sneaked into the hall and peeked around the corner. I moved and watched from place to place for hours. "Where is he?" I whispered to myself. "Does he see me moving from one hiding place to another? Is he also moving from one hiding place to another?" My hiding and moving maneuvers went on for the rest of the afternoon.

"What am I to do?" I finally whispered to myself. "Perhaps I need another revision."

My next revision was to stop moving and go back to my original plan of staying in one place until he showed himself. Behind L-Mom's lounge chair seemed like a good place to watch for him. Any thought of a catnap was definitely out of the question while this game of cat and lizard was happening.

Ole Alex strutted through the family room while I was peeking from behind the chair. He knew I was in big trouble. It was easy to tell he was gloating about it by the way he strutted. I hated to ask him for assistance, but I was getting desperate. As he came closer to me I whispered, "Alex, would you please hide here with me and help to watch for the sneaky little green lizard?"

Alex looked at me as though he didn't have the slightest idea about what I was asking. His up-bent whisker was waving around as he gave me his familiar sneer.

"I have more important things to do," he said while he self-importantly sashayed out of the room.

Afternoon turned into evening. I stayed crouched behind L-Mom's lounge chair. She and J-Dad watched television and later began to talk about going to bed. All of a sudden it happened! I saw him! The crafty little green guy dropped down from the green artificial palm tree in the corner of the room. No wonder I couldn't find him! His body color was exactly like the fake tree. I knew he had been laughing at me as I sneaked from one hiding place to another. He jumped down on the glass table filled with L-Mom's favorite seashells. She had lovingly gathered them from the New Jersey and Naples' beaches.

This was the moment I had been waiting for all day. My whiskers had not failed me. My plan, and its revisions, had worked. I sprang to my feet like never before and jumped up on the table with the lizard. The seashells flew all around on the tabletop. Some became airborne and were scattered across the floor as though the huge beach waves were once again in command of them.

L-Mom screamed when she heard the noise and saw her precious seashells falling to the floor.

"Twitter," she called, "what in the world is going on? Get down from there! Have you lost your mind?"

L-Mom never scolded me before, but she didn't know anything about the sneaky little green lizard, and I didn't have time to explain. I continued to frantically push those precious shells all over the table and onto the floor. I needed to keep searching for the lizard. I shoved away shells as L-Mom rushed over. Suddenly I saw him heading into a conch shell. I quickly put my paw on him. And just as quickly, he turned and ran. I was left with his tail still under my paw! He had escaped again!

L-Mom picked me up and said, "I can't imagine why you made such a mess Twitter."

I told her the whole story, and then she petted me and gave me one of her sweetest smiles.

She carried me over to J-Dad, deposited me in his lap, and went to the table to clean up my mess.

I lay there tired and totally defeated. J-Dad petted me and said, "Twitter, you had quite a time with the lizard. Don't worry about it. Tomorrow is another day. You can hunt for him then. L-Mom has wanted to rearrange those shells anyway."

I closed my eyes and a warm cozy feeling went all through my body. I like being on their laps. And I especially like it when they say such nice things to me. As I lay there, I remembered my feline Mom saying to me, "Flitter, all's well that ends in a well." Even though nothing ended in a well, my day was going to end *fairly* well. My thoughts went back over the day with the lizard and the foolproof plan my whiskers had told me to make. It was a wonderful plan and well executed, *as I see it.*

Suddenly, I came out of my reverie, and my eyes popped open. The more I thought about it, the more I realized I was not totally defeated. I sat up and shouted to the sneaky little green lizard, "Hey, little green lizard! Wherever you are! I know you are somewhere in here. Listen carefully. We are at war and will live to fight another day. Think about this! *I* won the battle today, because I still *have my* tail!"

Throwing down the gauntlet challenge to the lizard revitalized me, so I decided to work some more on my new invention. I jumped down from J-Dad's lap and began doing my warm-ups on the soft carpet. The first part of a warm-up is to lie down, turn on the left side, stretch the right paw high over the head, stretch the right leg out as far as possible, turn over to the right side, stretch the left side as the previous side, roll onto one's back, raise both front paws and hind legs into the air, wiggle and stretch, stand up and stretch one paw forward, then the other, and finish this abbreviated warm-up by alternating the back paws in the same manner.

I decided to go out on the pool patio. L-Mom was straightening up the seashells and soon they would be watching their favorite television shows. I like a calm, quiet, and peaceful atmosphere when I am inventing. It is a very attention demanding job. I must keep at it, because it will be so educational and healthy for the animal and feline community.

I then trotted out to the patio and saw Shuggy coming around the corner of the pool screen.

"Hey, good buddy," I shouted as I went up to the screen. We always get close together at the screen, because there is a lot of communication that goes on while just looking into each other's eyes. Besides, no one, especially Ole Alex, can hear what we are saying.

"Yo, Twitter," he said, "how goes it over here? Your Uncle Jerry and Aunt Vickie just came home. They let me out of the house to do my nighttime, outdoor, security patrolling. I thought I would take a peek over here first before I get formally started. How was your day?"

I told him all about the lizard experience and he said, "I'll bet you never see him again. Those sneaky little guys have a secret way of appearing and disappearing."

"I hope you are right. I wasted too much time today. I need to get on with my invention."

"What are you inventing?" Shuggy asked.

"My invention is officially named, *Animal's Aerobic Alphabetic Actions*. But it will commonly be called, *Twitter's Triple A*. It is a program both educational and health enhancing. I am now working on the 'J-K' action segment."

"Cool!" said Shuggy, "tell me all about it."

I answered in my formal speech style and recited the exact words which will be written in the instructional manual. "The actions go with the alphabet. They teach both parts to the participants. One starts with the 'A-B-C' action and progresses through the entire alphabet, thereby internalizing it. The healthy part of the program comes about by doing the actions that accompany each alphabetically named action. The two parts fit together very simply and perfectly."

I was delighted that he had asked, and I was happy to continue with my easy formal directions.

"I won't go into the warm-up exercises at this time," I began, "but one must always do them before doing any of the formal actions. The 'J-K' in the title of this one stands for Jump Kicking. It begins with one standing on one's hind legs, slowly bending one's knees while keeping one's balance, jumping high into the air, simultaneously kicking all four legs as vigorously as possible, and shouting the letters 'J-K.' Shall I demonstrate this alphabetic action for you?"

Shuggy cocked his head to one side and said, "Yeah, demonstrate it. I'm not quite sure I understood all those easy directions yet. A demonstration might help."

I took four deep breaths and said, "Shuggy, just the initial standing on one's hind legs part of this important exercise is healthy, because one must first of all be able to keep one's balance."

I then bent my legs, inhaled a deep breath and jumped straight up. While being airborne, I madly pawed the air with my front paws, kicked my legs every which way, shouted "J- K," and tried to do a twisting circle with my entire body. G-Ma, the twisting circle is not a formal part of this action, but I threw it in for Shuggy's sake.

"There you have it, Shuggy," I said, a little short of breath. "I'm sure you would enjoy it. I would be happy to teach the entire alphabet to you. Of course, I haven't finished inventing it yet. But, you could learn it as far as I've gone. You could practice the letters and actions while doing your nighttime security patrolling. And, we could even do them together when we have time."

"Yo, Twitter, that is really something. I think I could do the alphabet part, but I'm not sure I could master the actions the way you do them. I'll think about it. Now I have to go home and get busy."

Shuggy left to start his patrolling. I was tired from my day with the sneaky little green lizard but was pleased to have made progress with my invention by one more action.

Inside, L-Mom and J-Dad had shut off the television and were getting ready for bed. I needed to go inside in case they needed me for something.

I decided to lie down by the sliding glass door that leads out to the pool cage and watch for the sneaky green lizard. There was only a slight chance of seeing him, but I had nothing else to do yet.

J-Dad walked up to me and said, "Well, Twitter, we are going to bed now. It looks as if you are watching for your tailless lizard."

"Yes," I said, "I'm going to take catnap breaks with both eyes open all night."

J-Dad laughed a little and said, "That sounds like a good trick. I'll have to try it sometime."

I didn't know what he meant by a "good trick," but I would try to figure it out later.

I watched and watched for the lizard through the glass doors for a long time. The moon was shining brightly on the pool, and the filter circulated the water in little waves. It seemed as though the waves were doing a moonlight dance on the surface of the water. It was so peaceful and hypnotic. I could feel my eyes slowly going closed as my whiskers tried to alert me to another coming problem.

The next thing I knew, J-Dad was talking to me. I jumped to my feet and tried to open my eyes. They wouldn't open, but I could clearly hear J-Dad saying, "Twitter, you didn't bring any of your toys to our bedroom door. What happened to you last night? Did you watch for your lizard all night?"

I looked up at J-Dad through sleepy eyes and said, "One eye kept closing. Then the other eye closed, but I figured it would be all right because I still had my ears on alert status. I guess they must have closed too."

It was so strange, G-Ma. It was morning! I missed the entire night.

L-Mom and J-Dad went to work and Ole Alex is in the laundry room. He is still trying to stare a hole in the bathtub/laundry tub. I sneaked into the computer room to send you a morning e-mail. I will send you an update tonight about the latest warnings from my whiskers.

Love,
Twitter

CHAPTER 11

The Trip

Dear G-Ma,

I skipped your midnight e-mail last night because my day was unusually boring. The only important things were the constant warnings from my super-danger whiskers, and ominous feelings of an ill wind blowing my way.

Today, however, was a horrible day! It all started when I overheard J-Dad talking to you. I was crying huge tears and muttering to myself.

J-Dad looked down at me and said, "Twitter, what is wrong? Are you hurt?"

"My heart is broken," I sobbed, "G-Ma must not love me anymore!"

"Whatever gave you that idea?"

"I just heard you say G-Ma got a cat named Scan. That is a very important sounding name for a cat. She must not love me or need me anymore."

"Twitter, Twitter, of course she loves you. You have it all mixed up. You know G-Ma lives at the Carlisle. When one of the residents must go somewhere, either Clive or Lourdes takes them there. Clive picked up G-Ma yesterday in his big fancy bus and took her to Pro-Scan for a test. G-Ma got a cat-scan test and Clive took her back to her apartment. She was telling me all about the test and the good time they had. Clive picked her up early, drove very slowly, and took the long route to get there. He picked her up again when she was finished and took an even longer route to get back to her apartment. She thought he was lost when he drove half way to Marco Island, but he said she was his only passenger, and since they were having such good conversations, they might as well take a little joy ride. So you can relax Twitter. Your world did not come to an end."

Well, G-Ma, I was happy to know I was still your top-dog cat, but the relief it brought didn't eliminate the warning signals from my super-danger whiskers.

After I calmed down, I decided to go out on the pool deck and look for one of my good friends.

"There you are!" I said to the sun. "I really love you in the early morning! Of course I love you all during the day also, even when you try to hide my warm sunny spot on the family room carpet."

G-Ma, my good friend makes long shadows in the early morning for me. He makes me look like a tall skinny giant. I wave my paw, and my shadow waves back to me. Sometimes I turn half way around and wave my tail. It looks huge! I like to see it waving back to me. Whatever I do, my shadow does it too. Sometimes I run fast toward the glass doors and try to catch my shadow, but it climbs right up on the glass. One time I was running so fast I ran right into the glass door. I still run toward it, but now I stop just short of the door. I don't think I will ever be able to catch it. It doesn't matter because the game would probably be over if I did catch it.

I'll tell you a secret, G-M. I have to thank my good friend the sun for giving me the idea for my *Animal's Aerobic Alphabetic Actions* invention. One day, as I was out there jumping and cavorting around with my shadow, I realized what fun it was, and how healthy it would be for all the animals to learn some of my actions. I thought up the alphabet business all by myself though. Adding my alphabet component was sort of like creating one idea with two thoughts, *as I see it.*

I was playing with my shadow and thinking up more alphabet actions when Uncle Jerry and Aunt Vickie came in through the pool's screen door. "Hi, Twitter," Uncle Jerry said. "We didn't want to bother anyone, so we came around here to the back."

"Whoa," I said to myself as my whiskers began sending stronger warning signals, and I saw Uncle Jerry carrying Shuggy's car carrier! I wondered why were they bringing it over here without Shuggy? If Shuggy had to go somewhere, why couldn't Uncle Jerry or Aunt Vickie take him? If L-Mom or J-Dad had to take Shuggy somewhere, he could fit into my dreaded car carrier. These were very annoying questions, so I followed them into the house. Besides, it is my job to know what goes on around here in case anyone needs my help or advice.

Ole Alex was standing in the kitchen. He had a sneaky smile on his face. A smile on Ole Alex's face is always bad news. "Hellooow Twitter," he snarled to me. "How are you this glorious day?"

It was evident something was going on and I didn't know about it. It was also evident Ole Alex was way ahead of me in the information department. And, it was definitely evident Ole Alex was going to use it for all it was worth. I needed to play along with his little game to find the answer. I had an intuitive suspicion it had something to do with Shuggy's car carrier.

Uncle Jerry, Aunt Vickie, L-Mom, and J-Dad were chattering away in the kitchen. And there in the center of the kitchen was my dreaded car carrier sitting beside Shuggy's car carrier.

"Oh no!" I moaned. "Not that dreaded car carrier! I hate that thing!"

"You look a tad upset Twitter, my friend, whatever is the matter?" snarled Ole Alex.

I was more than a tad upset and I started blabbering, "I hate that thing. It is too dark in there. It is too small and the ceiling is too low. None of my toys are in there and I can't get a little sip of water. It even smells funny. L-Mom puts me in the front seat so I can look out at the big beautiful world, but I am still too low. I need a big pillow to boost me up, but I never get it. And then, the worse thing is, we have to go to Dr. Gomley's. He pokes, and looks everywhere, and then gives me shots. It's horrible!"

"Well, Twitter, my friend, I have excellent news for you," Alex said.

I calmed down a wee bit and began to assess the situation. Had I heard Ole Alex correctly? Had he said, "Twitter, my friend?" I think I remembered hearing it twice. Perhaps he had overcome his character flaw and was turning over a new whisker. That would be wonderful.

I cautiously asked, "Alex, what is your good news?"

Alex's eyes were again hooded as he answered, "Marianne used to take me in a car carrier all the time. It was loads of fun. We would go to the beach at Lowdermilk Park. I told Leslie all about it and she agreed to take us there. It will be a great adventure for you."

Well G-Ma, this was a change of character for sure. "Tell me all about it," I said.

"Yes, yes, I shall tell you all about it." Alex puffed up his chest and began to tell me about our upcoming adventure. "The beach is a wonderful place. There is sand everywhere. You can do anything you want to do in all that sand. We will be able to throw sand all around. We will walk to the water's edge and I will show you the little coquina-shell creatures. When the waves go out, those little guys squirm all about because they don't want to be uncovered. Then the waves come back and cover them up again. We can get our feet a little wet and catch them when the waves go out. They live in those tiny shells and try to burrow into the sand when they are uncovered. We can have a lot of fun scattering them all about."

I listened intently to Alex's story. I had never been to Lowdermilk Park, or any other beach for that matter, so I was eager to learn about it. I wasn't sure bothering those little coquina creatures was such a good thing, but I was eager to hear more about our adventure. "Go on Alex," I said.

"There are tall weedy looking things growing there called sea oats. No one is supposed to bother them, but we can sneak in and look for fire ants. They live in little sand hills. If you swat one of their hills, they all come out to greet you. Doesn't that sound good?"

I couldn't believe my ears. Ole Alex was being so nice. He must have planned this surprise with L-Mom. It seemed as though his bad character flaw had improved. What wonderful news! At last we could be friends and do a lot of good stuff together.

"When do we go?" I eagerly asked.

"You haven't heard it all yet, Twitter. People take all kinds of food and they drop it. It is there for the taking. Also, there is a lot of food by the trash barrels, because people toss good stuff at the barrels and miss. All you have to do is walk around and you will find a virtual smorgasbord," Alex continued.

This sounded wonderful; a great adventure and a new friend. L-Mom and J-Dad would also be happy about Alex loosing his nasty character flaw.

Alex was eager to tell me more. "There are also scads of sneaky little green lizards there too. Maybe you could practice your capturing skills and come up with something more than a dropped tail."

Well, G-Ma, that last remark caused me to stop and think a little. It sounded like something the old Alex would say. I thought perhaps he hadn't lost his entire character flaw yet. But still, the rest of his actions seemed to be a change in the right direction, so I decided to overlook his last remark.

Uncle Jerry and Aunt Vickie went home and left Shuggy's car carrier sitting in the kitchen right beside mine. L-Mom busied herself around the house for a while and I was getting anxious to get started on my adventure, so I followed her around and kept asking, "Are you about ready?"

L-Mom kept answering me with the same sentence, "Twitter, I have never, ever, seen you so anxious to get into your car carrier."

She finally finished with her busyness and we got into the car carriers. It was the first time in my whole life I didn't put up a terrible fuss about it. She zipped me in and immediately my super-danger whiskers alerted me. "Oh, no," I whispered to myself, "what could be wrong?"

L-Mom picked up my car carrier and carried me out to the car. My whiskers were demanding my attention, but I didn't know what was wrong. And even if I did know, there was nothing I could do while being zipped up in this dreaded car carrier. L-Mom opened the back door of her car and put me on the floor! "Hey" I shouted, "you made a mistake!" It was too late. The back door was shut and I was on the floor. It was dark back there. All I could see was the back of the front seat.

The other back door came open and J-Dad said, "In you go Alex." Apparently J-Dad had put Alex on the floor of the back seat too. Perhaps my whiskers were wrong and there was no danger after all. L-Mom opened the garage door and backed out. As soon as we were on our way, Ole Alex said, "Hey Twitter! You are in deep trouble this time."

"What do you mean?" I screamed.

Again Ole Alex was using his nasty voice as he said, "Today is *goodbye* Twitter. I won't have to see you ever again. I am taking over everything. The first thing I am going to do is lay claim to your warm sunny spot on the family room carpet."

"What are you talking about?" I shouted.

"We are not going to Lowdermilk Park. I made up that great story. We are headed to the animal shelter and L-Mom is going to leave you there. Do you know what they do to unwanted feral cats? It will be 'lights out' for you and good riddance."

I could not believe my ears. Ole Alex had lied to me about my adventure. Surely L-Mom was not going to abandon me. I started screaming and said, "L-Mom, I will bring more toys to your bedroom door every morning." I know she loves to pick them up and return them to my cut-down cardboard toybox. I screamed, "I will do double duty security patrolling. I will help J-Dad with more and more of his chores, and I will not let in any more sneaky little green lizards!"

I kept screaming and L-Mom said, "Twitter, be quiet. What in the world is wrong with you?"

Well, G-Ma, Ole Alex had really lied. We were just going to Dr. Gomley's for a checkup. When we got home, Ole Alex strutted off to try to stare his hole in the bathtub/laundry tub again.

I walked into the family room to look for my warm sunny spot on the carpet. I spotted it and shouted, "There you are! You are almost under the glass coffee table today." I wiggled around to get comfortable for a long catnap, but first I needed to decide if I should declare open warfare on Ole Alex or do as my Mom once said, "Give him enough rope." I didn't know how a rope would help, so I abandoned that idea. My eyes finally closed and my breathing became slower. I started to dream about a sneaky little green lizard's tail when all of a sudden my super-danger whiskers awakened me. They were alerting me to a danger from one of my own actions! Imagine that! One of my own actions was the cause of a coming problem! Nothing unusual happened the rest of the day, but I knew it would soon.

Love,
Twitter

CHAPTER 12

The Escape

Dear G-Ma,

I did my security patrolling all night and thought my hardest about a problem of my own making. There didn't seem to be an answer. Unbelievable!

Everything was in order this morning, so I went out on the pool patio. The sky was filled with white popcorn- shaped clouds that were hiding most of my good friend the sun. It is so much fun to watch the clouds make different shapes as they slowly move around in the sky. I love these relaxing Naples mornings especially after a long night of patrolling and hard thinking. My relaxation was soon ended, however, when Ole Alex came out on the patio. He walked up to me, stopped, and starred directly into my eyes. His one up-bent whisker was twitching wildly. It only took me an instant to ascertain he was still gloating about the Lowdermilk Park fiasco. We then had a starring contest for about five minutes. I was the winner, apparently, because Ole Alex was the first one to stop starring. He gave me his curled lip smile as he finally walked back into the family room.

Anyone could easily see Ole Alex was up to no good again. I watched as he looked all around the family room and finally spotted it. My friend, the sun, had skirted around the clouds and sneaked past the leaves of our lime tree to create a tiny, lacey, warm spot on the carpet for me. Alex looked back over his shoulder to make sure I was watching him and slowly made his way to my warm spot. He stretched out on my spot and again looked at me. It was a first class look of defiance. My tiny spot was much too small for Alex. I'm sure he didn't even want it. His actions were just to provoke me. After squirming around a little bit, Alex got up and headed for the laundry room. He was off to continue trying to stare a hole in his hated bathtub/laundry tub. He really hates his baths in there.

My whiskers had warned me of a coming problem of my own making. Alex's actions did not seem to be what it was, but since I couldn't deal with my unknown problem, I decided to keep my eye on Alex. Perhaps he was somehow connected to the coming problem. I hid behind the cooking island in the kitchen where he couldn't see me. I knew he wouldn't stare at the bathtub/laundry tub very long. He has hated the tub ever since he came to live here and found out L-Mom gives us baths in it. He still thinks his staring will create a hole in it. I should tell him it won't work, because I already tried it. But, it keeps him out of trouble.

Sure enough, after a short while, he came down the hall and cautiously looked around for me. I stayed hidden and he didn't see me. Alex quickly ran out to the patio and lay down next to the pool screen. It was strange behavior for Ole Alex because I had never seen him do it before. I whispered to myself, "Why would anyone in his right mind want to be squashed up against the screen like that?" His upper body was moving ever so slightly, and he kept looking over one shoulder for me. He was certainly going to cause some kind of trouble. Right then I remembered my Mom's words. She had said, "Flitter, whenever you see some kind of trouble brewing, you must nip it before it buds."

Heeding my Mom's advice, I nonchalantly strolled out onto the patio and totally ignored Ole Alex. I meandered around the pool deck as I got a little closer to him. I was nearly up to him before he saw me. All of a sudden his entire body stiffened as though he were frozen solid. Then I saw it! His right paw was on the outside of the screen! Alex had loosened the bottom of the screen and his front paw was entirely outside on the grass!

"Alex! What in the world are you doing?" I shouted.

He casually looked up and replied, "Not one little thing and it is none of your business."

"How did your paw get outside the screen?" I demanded in my most authoritative voice.

Ole Alex again looked defiantly at me and said, "It just happened to slip out as I was resting here."

It was immediately clear Ole Alex was trying to escape. A tiny opening in a screen can become a hole big enough for a cat to slip through to the outside. He had it all planned. He was going to escape!

And horror of horrors, it would be my fault, because it is my job to keep order and tight security around here.

"Get your paw back in here!" I demanded. Even though Alex is bigger than I am, he knows I have the highest authority around here because of two reasons. I have seniority and I am an adoptee instead of whatever Alex was at his Mom's cat shows. He also knows I have a leg up on him on the social ladder because of my adoptee attribute.

We had another staring match for about three minutes. Nothing moved in either of our bodies. He finally retracted his paw and sashayed off into the house as though nothing had happened. He did not even act guilty or remorseful. I decided right then and there to give him my executive silence for the rest of the day.

I tell you, G-Ma, it was one scary incident. How could I ever live with myself if he had finally made the hole large enough to escape? Poor L-Mom and J-Dad would cry a lot if they lost him. We had not even come close to correcting his character flaw or his one huge up-bent whisker. I would even cry a little too, because Alex needs a lot of my help in many areas. If we could change all the nasty things about him, he could be like all the other friends I have and love.

The popcorn clouds were much bigger now because they had joined together, and I could not see much of my warm sun. Since I couldn't play with my shadow, I made one more security check of the patio in case some bug, or ant, or sneaky little green lizard had found a way to get in. I told myself to watch Alex's hole in the screen and tell J-Dad about it when I found the time.

The warnings from my whiskers were still troubling me as I went into the family room. A danger from my own actions was on its way. "What in the world could it be?" I whispered to myself. "What have I done?" No answer came to my mind so I decided to work on my new invention.

I found a secluded place behind L-Mom's lounge chair. Being secluded is the best way to work on something. No one can bother you and you can concentrate much better. Besides, I don't want anyone to see any of the actions until they are perfected. Someone might want to try to improve part of the action. Once it is perfected, there is no way it *can* be improved. It is impossible to improve on perfection, *as I see it*. There is also the danger of Alex trying to steal my invention while it is still in the developmental stage. But no one else will be able to say they invented it, because when J-Dad invents his music, he fills out a paper that says, "no one can *copy*, or *write*, or lay claim to this work." He told me it is like a raincoat that protects you from the rain. I don't understand how a paper can protect you from the rain. J-Dad said he would help me get one of those paper raincoat protection papers that says "no one can *copy*, or *write*, or lay claim" to *my* invention.

I squirmed around on the carpet and did the entire necessary warm-up actions. Then I worked and perfected the next segment. Just as I finished, J-Dad came into the room and saw my tail sticking out from behind L-Mom's chair.

"What are you doing back there, Twitter?" he asked.

"I just finished the 'L-M' actions for my invention," I answered.

"Show them to me," he said.

"Okay," I gladly answered. I switched into my formal instructional voice and began reciting the actions, exactly as they will be written and protected by the "no one can *copy*, or *write*, paper."

"The 'L-M' position stands for 'Lunging Maneuvers.' Once one has done sufficient warm-ups, one stands erect on all four paws. One then begins the actions by putting one's left front paw forward as far as possible. Slowly bend one's right front knee to advance the lunge and begin repeating the letters 'L-M.' Lower the head to the floor to achieve more advancement of the lunging movement. Continue to bend the right knee as far as possible. Hold this completed lunging maneuver for at least five seconds. Take a big breath and prepare oneself for the next segment. One slowly returns to the stand-up starting position and repeats the lunging actions with the right front paw, all the while repeating the letters 'L-M' throughout this maneuver. These actions may be repeated as many times as one chooses, always trying to increase the repetitions to further one's health and alphabet knowledge."

I looked up at J-Dad with a happy grin on my face to see his reaction. I was very proud of my new invention and had worked hard on all the completed segments.

"That's pretty neat Twitter, keep it up," J-Dad said as he smiled and went off to his music room.

I was tired after all that inventing and needed a long catnap. It was a troubled catnap. The rest of the entire day was troubled because of my super-danger whisker warnings. They continued to demand my attention and alertness. All they would reveal to me was a coming problem caused by one of my own actions. Perhaps the answer will come tomorrow.

Love,
Twitter

CHAPTER 13

The Self-Made Problem

Dear G-Ma,

My day started with the absolutely catastrophic mystery about a problem of my own making. It was so disturbing. Everything seemed to be in perfect order all around the house. *As I see it,* my duty in life is to keep everyone to an orderly predictable routine and to keep everyone safe through my diligent security patrolling. Of course, there are secondary duties also, like being helpful, offering advice when I see the need, and trying to cure Ole Alex's character flaw. And I do them with great dedication and satisfaction. And, I would be the last one to brag, but I think I do a pretty good job of it too. So, the question remains, what problem of my own making is worrying my whiskers?

L-Mom went shopping this morning, and J-Dad was making noise in his music room. Ole Alex was in the laundry room. He was still trying to stare a hole in the bathtub/laundry tub so it wouldn't hold his bath water. Everything seemed to be under control, so I decided to go play with my shadow on the pool patio. As I stepped through the sliding glass doors, I was disappointed to find humungous cotton ball clouds in the sky. They were hiding the sun: one of my best friends. That eliminated my shadow playing this morning. I needed to work some more on my invention anyway. I began with my warm-ups on the little rug in front of the screen door and worked on the 'N-O-P' actions until they were perfected. I was tired, so I decided to rest and watch all the different kinds of birds that visit our back yard.

I got comfortable on the little rug and saw Shuggy rushing around the corner of our house. He always runs wherever he goes. That must be why he is so skinny. "Yooo, Twitter, what's going on at the Spiess residence today?" he panted as he ran up to the screen.

"Hi Shuggy," I said. "I just finished another segment of my invention and was resting and watching all the birds. Did you ever notice the ones up there on the telephone wire? Some face one way and the others face the opposite way. Why do they do that? Maybe some want to see where they have been, and the others want to decide where they will go when they leave."

Shuggy said, "Nope, never paid much attention to them. Did you ever eat one?"

"*Eat* one? Why would I *eat* one?"

"I thought all cats ate birds. Don't you?"

Those were startling words: an absolutely unthinkable concept. "Well, *I* never did," I said, "the only time I was close to one was when I was very little and up a tree in the foggy woods. A horrible big buzzard bird up there wanted to eat *me*. That was before I was rescued and became an adoptee. Some of the birds out there hop around on the grass and eat bugs and ants. I certainly wouldn't want to eat anything that eats bugs and ants!"

"Anyway," I continued, "I like to watch and listen to them. Some like to sit on the roof of our shed in the far back yard, and some hide from something in our lime tree. There are big birds that sort of cackle when they talk and little birds who just chitter-chatter. Some make their voices go up and down. I tried to talk to them one time, but I guess they didn't understand my Felinese language."

"I heard on television that birds go way up North in the summer," I said, "maybe they speak Canadianese. It'd be cool to learn it and talk to them. I'm sure they know all sorts of good stuff."

"I remember, Shuggy," I continued, "one time my Mom told me that if I ever had two birds in the bush it was better than having one in my hand. But I never went into any bushes to look for those two birds. Sometimes they come close to the pool screen. I sit very still so as not to frighten them and I get a good look at them. They have beautiful colors and tiny piercing eyes. And they also have those funny spindly legs and toes. How in the world can those skinny legs hold them up? And especially since they have only two of those funny legs. Sometimes a lot of them are all flying around in a big circle like a huge umbrella. I wonder if they get dizzy."

"Yeah, probably," said Shuggy. "When I chase my tail around in a circle, I get dizzy."

"The best thing about birds, though, is that they can fly. How did their Moms teach them to do it? I've tried jumping off the patio table and madly kicking all four legs, but I just go straight down and hit the pool deck every time. I wish my Mom had taught me to fly. Have you ever tried it Shuggy?"

"Nope, I never even thought about trying to fly."

"Sometimes a whole flock is under our lime tree. They eat the fallen rotten limes and then dance all around. My feline Mom said to me once, 'Flitter, I want you to always remember something.' I said, 'Yes, I will always remember something.' Then she said, 'Birds with one feather flock together.' I keep watching, but I never see a whole flock, or even a single bird, with only one feather. Have you ever seen one?"

"Nope," said Shuggy. "Never saw a flock or a single bird with only one feather. Sometimes I see only one feather on the ground, but the bird has disappeared. Hey, what's the new segment you just perfected?"

I switched into my formal voice and began reciting the words as they will be written and protected by the paper raincoat.

"The 'N-O-P' position," I began, "stands for 'Nose Over Paws.' Once one has done one's warm-ups, one gets down on the floor on one's stomach. The front paws are then stretched out as far as they will go. One then raises one's hips upward and stretches one's body forward and toward the right paw. One tries to position one's nose over one's right paw, all the while repeating the letters, 'N-O-P.' One returns to the starting position and repeats the action with the left paw. One then sits upright and extends the right back paw forward to the front and to its fullest extent. Lastly, bend forward at the waist and extend one's nose as close to the right back paw as far as possible. Sit back up, return the paw to the body, and repeat the action with the left back paw and nose. This action may be repeated as many times as one chooses, always trying to increase the repetitions to further one's health and alphabet comprehension."

"That's really great Twitter. You might become famous with your invention," Shuggy said. "I'm going to get into all that stuff when you get it finished."

"Well, Shuggy," I said, "I'm not really inventing this program to get famous. I just feel that education and good health are very important. L-Mom tries to keep us all healthy. She is always giving me vitamins and health food. She also gives me a few Frisky Feline Fish Morsels for a treat. But, most animals are not as lucky as I am, so they need some kind of health guide. My invention will be a good beginning for them."

"You're right as usual Twitter," Shuggy said. "I have to get back home now and check on your Aunt Vickie and Uncle Jerry. Hey! I just thought of something! We must be cousins!"

"I don't know much about cousins, Shuggy. My feline Mom once told me something about 'kissing cousins,' but she didn't say we had to go around kissing to be one. I hope not. I don't think we should be kissing. Maybe there are all kinds of cousins. Why don't you ask my Aunt Vickie and Uncle Jerry about it?"

Shuggy took off and ran home. I hope he finds out we are not the kissing kind of cousin, because I'm not too keen on kissing Shuggy.

As I went back into the house, Ole Alex was coming from the laundry room. He had the same old scowl on his face. I decided to try to help his character flaw by suggesting something.

"Hi Alex," I said. "I just finished a segment of my 'Animal's Aerobic Alphabetic Actions' program. As you may or not know, it has an educational component. I get a lot of my education from watching television. There are scads of programs about all kinds of subjects. It is not as good for learning things as it is from learning things from a computer, but it is a close second."

G-Ma, as soon as I mentioned the computer, I could have kicked myself. If anyone ever "left the cat in the bag," I just did. Fortunately, my mistake slipped right past him. My nighttime computer activities and e-mailings to you have to be *our* little secret.

I quickly continued with my idea of trying to interest Ole Alex in education. "Alex, you could learn lots of intellectual stuff from the television. I watch J-Dad's car races with him for hours and hours. He thinks I'm still watching even though I take long catnaps on his lap. When J-Dad has to go somewhere during a race, he saves the rest of the race inside the television somewhere. Sometimes he has the television save the entire race inside of it. Then, we watch it at another time. I am not fond of watching the cars race for hours, but it is a wonderful time for the two of us to be together. We get to do a lot of male bonding."

"Some nights I sit on L-Mom's lap to watch her programs. L-Mom has a different style of television watching. I call it the 'up and down' style. We watch for a short while, and then L-Mom says, 'down you go Twitter. I'll be right back.' L-Mom then jumps up and hurries off to do something. 'Okay, Twitter,' she says as she settles back down into her lounge chair, 'let's watch some more of our cooking show.' I jump back up and get myself comfortable, but soon L-Mom jumps up again. She's off to do another chore. It goes on that way all evening. The best 'up and down' is when she goes to the kitchen and makes our television-watching popcorn. I need lots of sips of water then because the popcorn is salty. Then I have to use L-Mom's 'up and down style' too."

Alex continued to listen, so I went on about the advantages of watching television. "Sometimes I like to watch from the top of the glass coffee table. I am closer to it, and there is a lot of room to spread out or change positions. It doesn't really matter where you watch, Alex, the important thing is you can learn a lot."

I thought this might be a good opportunity to add a little something about interpersonal relationships, so I said, "You can see how nicely the people talk and act toward each other."

"The colors are also very beautiful. If there is some kind of talking or action program that J-Dad and L-Mom do not like, they just push a button and it is gone. I would be happy to inform you when a nice program is showing, and help you find a comfortable place to watch with us if you would like."

Alex continued to look at me. His expression did not change, but he said, "I'll think about it."

I considered that to be a great victory. Perhaps we can change his character flaw after all.

Well, G-Ma, for the rest of the day, my whiskers continued to warn me about the problem of my own making. And they added some new information. They indicated that you were also involved! The whole thing seems so preposterous. A problem of my own making! What is it? Why didn't it present itself all day? A great deal of my life is dedicated to solving problems, not making them. The mystery must be solved tomorrow!

Love,
Twitter

CHAPTER 14

The Critical Hacker

Dear G-Ma,

My Mom once told me, when we all lived in our cozy cut-down cardboard box by the lady's back door, "Flitter, you are going to be super special when you grow up, someone who is loving, and kind, and wants to solve problems. But you also may have to solve problems that you create yourself. It's the way life is, *as I see it.*"

The last thing in the world I ever wanted to do was create a problem for our wonderful family. As you know, when J-Dad is home, I follow him around the house all day. Wherever he goes, I'm right there in case he needs to talk with me, or needs help or advice. I also check in with L-Mom frequently to remind her of my availability. In my spare time, I do the daytime security patrolling, catnapping, and the *Animal's Aerobic Alphabetic Actions* inventing. My agenda also allots time to try to think of ways to help Ole Alex's character flaw problem; the one that is evidenced by his one up-bent whisker. It is important for me to be aware of all events going on around here so I can keep a leg up on everything. It is my mission in life, and my self-assigned duty *as I see it.* And yet, here I am being warned about a problem of my own creation. Unbelievable!

J-Dad spends a lot of time making noise while inventing his music and a lot of time computing in the office. I sit on his lap when he does these things so I can be available for whatever he might need. My own computing skills started as I intently watched the computer action. The gadget called a "mouse" interested me at first, but it soon became evident it was totally misnamed.

Everything about the computing process intrigued me. The keys made an interesting little noise, and the screen showed letters that were just like the keys. Sometimes there were pictures and sounds. The screen was in constant motion. It was difficult to know whether to watch the keys or the screen.

To get a better look, I began watching from the desktop. Most of the time J-Dad seemed to enjoy this computing thing, but once in a while he would say, "Oh no!" or, "Oh nuts." Those words didn't explain much to me. After many hours of watching, I decided I had to learn how to do this computing thing too. Little did I know there were dangers associated with a computer!

Night after night I spent hours on the desktop. It took many false attempts to find the right thing to do to turn it on. When it finally came on, the start-up sound nearly scared me out of my tiger striped fur. Very gingerly I touched one of the keys but nothing happened. The next attempt had the same result; nothing happened. I knew then why J-Dad said, "Nuts" so often. The thing seemed to have a mind of its own. In desperation I pranced around on those keys with all four paws. Nothing happened, so I got back on the desktop. Then it happened! I accidentally bumped the mouse gadget. Lo and behold, something moved on the screen. What fun it was! Just move the mouse gadget and an arrow moved around on the screen. I also discovered I could prance around on the keys while twitching my tail on the mouse gadget to make the arrow move.

As you know, G-Ma, it took a lot of watching J-Dad, to get to the point in my education where I actually conquered the computer. The important thing to remember was to use the side of my paw with a gentle tap on only one key at a time. My greatest victory was learning to do the e-mail stuff and becoming proficient enough to write my letters to you. That was a long time ago and all the while I was unaware that a cyber disaster lay ahead.

It finally happened tonight. I went into the office at midnight to send you my daily e-mail letter and there it was! The problem of my own making was staring at me. It was right there on the computer screen! I knew you couldn't hear me, but I shouted anyway, "Help! G-Ma! Call the FBI! Call the police and the computer cops!" My hard-earned computing skill, of which I am very proud, was the problem of my own making. I never receive any e-mail because I only send to you. And, I know you would return e-mail if you knew how to make a computer do the sending stuff instead of just finding mine in the sky and putting it in one of the computers in your computer room. But, I do have an e-mail address. All of us accomplished computer users do. It is just part of the computer education process.

Anyway, as I opened my e-mail site tonight there was a letter from some Elliot-dude! My computer had been hacked! The Elliot-dude had read all my letters to you. He knows all my thoughts and everything. He even horribly criticized my writing. He read the e-mail letter which explained how I became an adoptee and said it needed, "forward looking suspense!" The Eliot-dude then proceeded to rewrite the whole account of the event. The Elliot-dude changed my story by saying some dog cut me off as I headed for the safety of the friendly tree, and he changed it to say I had to make a diversion to get to safety. He said his added diversion would make my story have a lot more of his "forward looking suspense!" How dare he take the truth and change it? The Elliot-dude wasn't even there! He wants me to put in stuff that didn't happen! When I have something to say, I believe in just simply saying it. As you know, I like to keep things simple. There is no need to embellish a simple factual sentence, or thought, or story, or anything.

This Elliot-dude said he knows how to write properly because he writes *math* books. What is math anyway? *As I see it,* it's just a bunch of numbers. My Mom taught me all about arithmetic. First she said I needed to learn to count up things as far as I wanted to go. So I learned to count up all the things in our cozy cut-down cardboard box and a few more imaginary things. Then Mom said I needed to learn how to count down. She said it was important because if I had some things, and then I didn't have all of them, I needed to count down in order to know exactly how many things I actually had. After I learned all about up and down arithmetic, Mom said I should learn some higher up stuff too. It was called the "ga-zinduz." Mom said if she gave me nine treats and asked me to share with Gomer and Harold, I would have to know how many times three ga-zinda nine. I worked on that problem for a long time and finally told her I would just pass out the treats until they were gone. Mom said my arithmetic was sufficient and we would forget all about math.

The Elliot-dude's *math* has nothing to do with my letters to you or my adoptee story. *Math* has nothing to do with J-Dad, L-Mom or you. It has nothing to do with my job around here trying to keep a safe and orderly household. And besides, who needs more *math* books? *Math* never changes! One and one are always two. The only person who needs a math book is someone who can't remember things very well. Most of us don't even *need* a math book!

I talked to L-Mom this morning, in an indirect way about computer viruses. I didn't want her to know I had been messing with the computer because she might not approve, but she just sweetly said, "Twitter, you don't need to worry about such things. I don't think there is anything wrong with our computer. Sometimes you make much ado about nothing."

I was still worried about the Elliot-dude though. His spying had to stop; one-way or the other. I thought perhaps J-Dad might have an answer. I didn't hear any guitar noise coming from his music room, but I started looking for him in there anyway. Sure enough, he was in there, but he was not making any noise. He was just holding his guitar and staring off into space.

"What are you doing, J-Dad?" I asked.

"Hi Twitter," he said. "I'm not doing anything."

"Well, when you finish doing nothing will you let me know? I have something very important to tell you."

J-Dad laughed for some reason and said, "Let's have a go at it, Twitter."

I didn't know what he was talking about, so I jumped up on his lap and started telling him my concern. "I think it is very likely someone has hacked into the computer." I was very careful to say, *"the"* computer instead of *"our"* computer. It was clever of me to catch it, and it took a little bit of quick thinking to avoid that big mistake. Maybe J-Dad and L-Mom wouldn't care if I used the computer, but at this point, the main thing to do was get rid of the Elliot-dude.

J-Dad asked, "Whatever makes you think such a preposterous thing?"

"Sometimes when I am patrolling and guarding the house at night, there is a noise coming from the computer." I truthfully continued, "I therefore concluded it was being used, and you should make sure nothing terrible is happening." That was a tiny little stretch of the truth, but it was sorely needed.

J-Dad could see I was extremely upset so he said, "Twitter, I'm sure I know who is creating the noise, and I will install a new security system in it. Will that calm you down and make you happy?"

Well, G-Ma, my self-made computer problem would be solved with the new security system, and it will be the end of the Elliot-dude. But my super danger whiskers are alerting me to one of the biggest problems I have ever faced. I hope I am still alive tomorrow night to contact you!

Love,
Twitter

CHAPTER 15

The Beauty and the Beetle

Dear G-Ma,

L-Mom went to her office this morning and J-Dad went to Fort Myers to fix the television station again. All was secure on the home front, so I went into the family room to work on my *Animal's Aerobic Alphabetic Actions* invention. I looked all around and finally said, "There you are!" My warm sunny spot was playing a game of hide and seek with me again. It was almost under L-Mom's shell table. I jumped on it and wiggled all around. I love my warm sunny spot! Then I got on my back, put all four paws into the air, shut my eyes, and put on my creative thinking cap.

Creative thoughts were swirling all around in my head when I was interrupted by a growling voice saying, "What are you supposed to be doing?"

I opened one eye and looked up to see Ole Alex standing there. His eyes were half closed. He looked like an alligator eyeballing a small dog on a canal bank.

"I'm doing some creative thinking for my invention," I quietly said. "Is something wrong?"

"There is always something wrong. I just wanted to remind you that I am known as a pedigreed, beautiful, Long Haired White. Do you know what you are? You are an unbeautiful, feral, short haired, skinny, tiger runt!"

"Alex, what are you talking about? I said as I sprang to my feet.

"I'm talking about us. My Mother was a winner in cat shows and I look just like her. The favorite color of the judges is white. I am all white except for a big beautiful complimentary tan tail. And I have tan accents on top of my head. The only white fur you have is an extremely modified, triangular napkin-shape on your chest and some white on your left front paw. And the white on your left paw is even marred by a very small scraggly circle of coal black fur."

Well, G-Ma, Alex was certainly in a bad mood. I never intended to embarrass him by bringing up any more of my wonderful past, especially since I am an adoptee. An adoptee is the greatest thing to be, *as I see it.* Just the mention of it could hurt his feelings, but it seemed as though he needed to be enlightened a little more on a few other topics.

"Now hold on Alex," I said. "My feline Mom was a beautiful tiger cat and she was very smart too. She knew everything there was to be known about everything. She told me lots of good stuff to always remember, and I promised to remember it. Sometimes I forget a little of it though. She told Gomer, and Harold, and me, how very lucky we all were. And she told us everything there was to know about beauty too. I loved the beautiful old towels in the bottom of our cozy cut-down cardboard box and could hardly wait to see the big beautiful outside world she told us about."

I took a deep breath and continued. "Mom told Gomer he was a gorgeous black kitten whose fur looked like a raven flying in the sunlight, and his four white paws were a superb contrast. Mom said some lucky owner would probably change his name to 'Boots.' Mom told Harold he was as handsome as his father, because Harold had the same large brownish splashes mixed in with his black fur. He also had the same tiny white hairs sprinkled around his face. She said those same white hairs were just enough to make Harold look handsome and distinguished."

I was on a roll, so I kept on rolling. "Mom told me I looked so much like her we could be twins. I could see how my tiger stripes matched Mom's tiger stripes. There was one tiny difference between us though. As you have noticed, I do have a very teeny circle of black fur in a field of white on my left front paw. I pointed it out to Mom once and she said, 'Sweetheart, that is your beauty mark, as if you need anything to point to your beauty.'"

"I don't understand about a beauty mark," I said to Mom.

"A beauty mark is a special thing," she said. "Regular beauty is only as deep as your skin. That beauty mark indicates your beauty goes deeper than your skin. It is deep inside you and shows that you are a beautiful creature inside and out."

G-Ma, I totally didn't understand how anyone could see inside you, and I also didn't understand what was inside of me that could be beautiful. But if Mom said so, it had to be true.

I continued to explain my beauty mark to Alex. "My Mom said, 'Your beauty mark points to your honesty and love of everything and everyone. It points to your desire to be helpful, courageous, and diligent in all you will ever do. Cherish your beauty mark, Flitter, and always be proud of it.'"

"I still think it is a defect!" Alex said as he sashayed down the hall to the utility room. He stopped just long enough to look at me over his shoulder and say, "And I think the lady left open the door on her porch for one reason. And the reason was to get rid of you!"

Poor Alex. He always looks on the bad side of everything. There has to be something more I can do to help change his character flaw. I need to work on his problem soon.

Well, G-Ma, Ole Alex totally destroyed my creative juices. There was no way I could get back into a relaxed frame of mind to concentrate on my invention. The end of the alphabet is so near at hand and the animal world needs my invention so badly. In my mind's eye, I dream of all the animals getting healthier, and having fun with all the actions. I know how much more they will appreciate our wonderful world when they have mastered our alphabet and can put it to work for them. Having an education is like opening the door to everything.

The rest of my day was spent doing routine things like patrolling, catnapping, helping J-Dad with his guitar noise when he came home, and watching L-Mom puttering around after she came home. Later we had our evening popcorn and television programs before bedtime. I was hoping for a calm night of security patrolling, but it was not to be. Once again my super-danger whiskers alerted me to an immediate problem happening in our house! I need to get a little sip of my water and I'll be right back to tell you.

After everyone was asleep, I went into the laundry room and there it was! A black beetle ran out from under the washing machine and was scurrying across the tile floor.

"Hey, what are you doing in here?" I said in my most authoritative voice. "You can't be in here. How did you get in here? Where do you think you are going? Stop right where you are!"

The little black beetle never answered me. He kept right on scurrying across the floor.

"Hey you, stop! You can't be in here! I'm in charge of patrolling to make sure everything is as it should be. I have rules. I don't allow any kind of beetle in this house!"

G-Ma, the little black beetle paid no attention to me! He kept scurrying across the floor. I chased after him and batted at him with my paw. He flew across the floor and landed on his back, but quickly righted himself and headed back toward the washing machine. I had to act quickly. If he crawled under it, I could lose him forever.

My back legs sprang into action and propelled me in his direction. I batted at him again. It slowed him down and I captured him under my front paw. I held him down for a while. I think I knocked the wind out of him, because when I lifted my paw to look at him, he didn't even move one hairy leg. I nudged him a little. He still didn't move. I thought it would be a good idea to bat him around a little more anyway. I even tossed him in the air a few times. After the last toss, he landed on his back and those creepy hairy legs stuck straight up into the air. Actually, two of his hairy legs had come off and landed over by the clothes dryer. I decided to leave him in the middle of the room to make it easier for L-Mom to find him in the morning.

Ole Alex came sashaying into the laundry room as I was leaving. I sensed trouble because he usually sleeps all night. He lowered his head and stared at me with half-closed eyes. His curled up lip made a nasty sneer as he said, "Hey, how many lives do you have left?"

"What are you taking about?" I said.

"I asked you how many lives you have left. Cats only have nine lives. How many do you have left?"

"I never heard of such a thing. If it is true, then I guess I have all nine."

Alex kept staring at me: the stare he uses to make a hole in the bathtub/laundry tub. He wasn't making a hole in me either, but he said, "I have all nine of mine. You have used up most of yours. You probably only have one half of your last life left!"

"What?" I screamed. I didn't know anything about any nine lives business. My Mom once told me cowards died many times, but she said I didn't have to worry because I was brave.

Alex's up-bent whisker was waving in my face as he said, "The way I figure it, remember in your life history lessons, you told me about escaping up the tree from the barking dog? There went your life number one. And the story about the buzzard that almost killed you? I figure you lost another life there. I count it as life number two. Then there was a black ghost that was going to eat you? Whoever heard of a black ghost anyway? Count that as life number three gone down the drain. And I clearly remember your panic attack and fright when you thought you were going to be dumped off for good at the vet's instead of a glorious day at Lowdermilk Park. That escapade counts as life number four. Do you see how close you are to the end of your life, old buddy? Let me continue. I clearly recall your horrendous day chasing the poor little green lizard, and all you had to show for it was a detached tail. You used up life number five on that big deal. And all that inventing nonsense you do counts as life number six. Remember the night of the big party when you were shut up in the guest bedroom all night? All your fretting and fussing about it surely cost another one. Say goodbye to life number seven. Then there was the deal on the patio when a poor little lizard was in the plant and you upset the watering pail and nearly drowned yourself. Boy that cost you another one. We are up to number eight now. Throw in a few more odds and ends and I figure you are down to about one half of one life left."

Alex stopped talking, but continued to stare at me. He was waiting for my reaction. I finally composed myself and said, "My feline Mom never told me anything about nine lives."

"Well, that's just too bad. Have you made out your will? You don't actually need a will, because you don't have anything anyway except your exalted place in this household. And I will soon be taking over that position when your one half a life is used up."

Alex strutted away toward the family room again and I stood there in a most bewildered state. I wondered if he had told the truth, and if there was such a thing as nine lives. L-Mom would have to help me with this problem, and I needed to find ways to help change Alex's character problem.

Well, G-Ma, midnight seemed to come early tonight with all the beetle and Alex business. It will also be a short night tonight. The person who runs the world made everyone change all the clocks. And then, everyone has to do the changing all over again sometime later. It is either forward or backward- again and again. Everyone's schedule has to keep changing because of the rule.

My good friend, the sun, doesn't like the rule either because he has to chase away the darkness one hour earlier. Ever since forever, the sun had a definite schedule. Now the schedule has to be changed. I end up with shorter catnaps, and our meals are off schedule. My tummy is small, and an hour longer to wait for dinner is a long time. I wish I could talk to the person responsible for all the changing. I would explain all the problems and get the rule thrown away. Then time would just go on and on in a straight line and not jump forward or backward.

I would like to tell the person who runs the world that if a schedule is in place, and it is a good one, there is no need to make a rule that keeps changing it. My experience has taught me to think very carefully before making a rule, and once you make it, you stick to it. That is the way it should be, *as I see it*. Besides, I like to keep things simple.

Tomorrow will be a busy day. I need to talk to L-Mom about my nine lives, work on Alex's problem, and try to finish my invention. I think I need an assistant. Oh no! My super-danger whiskers just started alerting me to something horrible headed my way. I'll tell you all about it tomorrow night at midnight.

Love,
Twitter

CHAPTER 16

The Funeral

Dear G-Ma,

One of the most horrible things in the world happened to me last night after I sent you my midnight e-mail. I walked into the kitchen to get a little sip of water. I looked down at my water dish and shouted, "Oh no!" Floating in my drinking water was poor Billy: my favorite red, toy, catnip mouse. His whole body was swollen with water. Poor Billy! I gently scooped him out with my paw and placed him on the floor. His smell was even gone. My best friend was drowned and murdered. My entire tummy felt as though it had a big hole in it. I got down beside him and my tears joined the water that was leaking out of him.

"Billy," I quietly said, "can you still hear me? Do you know you are dead?"

Billy didn't move. His puddle just got bigger. My security patrolling was done rapidly all night so I could spend my time with Billy. Even if you are dead, it's nice to have someone with you, *as I see it.*

I could hardly wait for J-Dad and L-Mom to get up this morning. L-Mom is home on Saturdays and has more time to talk to me about things. She knows all about all kinds of stuff. My feline Mom told me to always have a pinch whenever I needed a substitute, so J-Dad is my substitute pinch when L-Mom isn't here. We needed to talk about Billy, and the nine lives business, and about more help correcting Alex's character flaw.

"L-Mom, hurry," I said as she came out of their bedroom and began picking up my delivered toys. "I need to talk to you."

"My goodness," she said. "You certainly are all fired up this morning. What is wrong now? Did another beetle get into the laundry room?"

She continued to walk toward the kitchen and I followed as closely as possible. Sometimes I was even ahead of her. "Alex is fixated on death." I shouted. "And he said I started with nine lives but only have half a life left! How long is half a life? And he killed poor Billy! He drowned him in my water dish! Billy's catnip smell is even gone. What am I going to do?" I wailed.

By then we were in the kitchen and L-Mom could see poor Billy by my water dish. Billy had a bigger puddle of water surrounding him now, and he was still leaking. Big tears were running down my cheeks, and they splashed in Billy's puddle. I started hiccupping in between my sobs. It was awful!

L-Mom picked me up and gave me lots of love-petting. It helped a little. Then L-Mom said, "Twitter, this was a naughty thing done to Billy, and you don't have to worry about the nine lives business. It was just a tale told to you by Alex and signifying nothing. It's called a 'figure of speech.' There is no truth to it at all."

"I didn't know speech had figures," I sniffled. "I'm glad I didn't have to put any speech figures in the directions of my *Animal's Aerobic Alphabetic Actions* invention."

"Did you know Billy was a twin?" L-Mom said. "I know a store where his twin lives. I could go there and ask his twin to come and live with us. Then you will have a new toy mouse. He even smells like Billy. Would you like me to do it?"

I stopped sniffling and said, "I would love it! I'll name him Billy Two. He can be my new favorite red, toy, catnip mouse. It will be almost as good as still having Billy with me!"

L-Mom put me down and got some paper towels to clean up Billy's leaks. Then she picked him up in a dry paper towel and gently put him in the kitchen sink. "Twitter," she said, "I think we need to put more effort into helping Alex with his character problems. Do you think you can do that?"

I thought about L-Mom's request and remembered my feline Mom telling me to turn all the stones over to look for a solution to a problem. I am not allowed outside to turn over any stones, but I told L-Mom I would work on it and think of something. I did however, have a big favor to ask L-Mom.

There was still a little sniffle in my voice as I said, "L-Mom, may we have a funeral for poor Billy?

I really want him to have a proper funeral, and everyone should be invited. Shuggy would be hurt if we had a funeral and didn't invite him. And Uncle Jerry and Aunt Vickie would want to come too. We should bury Billy out under the lime tree where I could almost see him every day. Our lime tree would be honored to be part of Billy's funeral. It could wave its leaves over Billy just like it waves to me."

I didn't have any sniffles in my voice any more because I was so excited. My brain kept making more and more plans for the funeral. I said, "Alex and I could get into our dreaded cat carriers and J-Dad could carry us out under the lime tree. I will compose an *Ode to Billy* and conduct the whole thing. Billy would love it. It's the least we can do since he was drowned and murdered."

L-Mom looked at me, smiled, shook her head, and said, "That is a lovely idea Twitter."

Later, everyone followed my plans and gathered under our lime tree. My good friend, the sun, sent tiny little sparkling rays down through the leaves to call attention to its presence. I cleared my throat and started the ceremony by saying, "Friends, relatives, we have come to bury Billy and to praise him." The rest of the ceremony went as planned and was completed when I recited my heartfelt composition.

My Ode to Billy
Dear Billy. You were my favorite toy.
I loved your catnip smell.
I'm sorry you got wet, and ruined,
and leaked a puddle on the kitchen floor.
I didn't want to throw you in the trash,
so we are putting you here under the lime tree.
I hope that is all right with you.
Goodbye,
Twitter and the rest of your family.

It was the proper thing to do *as I see it.*

My next job was to turn my attention to Ole Alex, since I promised L-Mom I would work on his character flaw. He was very solemn all during the funeral. No one mentioned the drowning or murder to him. We are hoping he will realizes how much love we have to give to everyone and everything connected to us. We want to love him too if he will allow it. Perhaps today will be the beginning of a complete turnaround for him.

Well, G-Ma, after all the funeral activities, I began thinking about all the other work I had to do. When J-Dad is home, I need to help with his music noise, and be available to give advice when he is doing other activities. And I need to deal with this entire nine lives and murder business stuff. Then there is Billy Two moving in, and finding time to put more effort into helping correct Alex's character flaw. My poor neglected invention needs a lot more work too. Thinking about all of this work nearly wore me out. I decided I definitely needed a long catnap to get rejuvenated.

As I headed into the family room, I looked all around for my warm sunny spot. It was not there. Apparently some huge dark clouds had once again filled our Naples' summer sky with a promise to unload some more rain. The next best place for a long catnap is in J-Dad's lounge chair. I jumped up into it and squirmed all around until I got completely comfortable. Just then Alex walked into the room. Remembering my promise to L-Mom, I said, "Hi Alex. Would you like to join me up here for a long catnap? The funeral must have worn you out too."

Alex stood there looking at me for a while and finally said, "No, but thank you anyway."

Wow! It was the first time I ever heard Alex thank anyone. I was glad he didn't want to join me in the chair, because I like to stretch out over the whole cushion. Maybe he knew there wouldn't be enough room for the two of us to be comfortable. I hope he appreciated the offer though.

For some reason I could not get in ten winks of a short catnap so I decided to work on my long neglected invention. I jumped down on the carpet and wiggled all around. I stretched and did some deep breathing before going through the necessary warm-up activities. The last thing I needed today was muscle cramps to slow me down. Once my muscles were warmed up, I thought and thought about the next segment. I was up to the 'U-V-W' segment. I had it all worked out for the 'U.' I wanted it to be dynamic, so I am using the word 'ultimate.' But I was totally stuck on the 'V' position and its actions.

Alex sashayed back into the family room about then and came close to me. He looked at me on the floor and asked, "What are you doing now, Twitter?"

"Oh, hello Alex," I answered, "I'm trying to work out the 'V-W' parts for a segment of my invention. I'm having a lot of trouble with it. All the other letters and actions were much easier. Not that they were easy, because they were a lot of work, but for some reason I am stuck on this one."

Alex stood there looking at me for a while. Then he screwed up his face and turned his head from one side to the other. It was obvious he had a dilemma. Finally he looked straight at me and said, "I can help."

"Am I hearing things?" I whispered to myself. "Is Alex offering to help me?"

"That would be wonderful." I said. "What did you have in mind?"

Alex took a deep breath. He hesitated. This was new territory for him and he didn't know how to proceed. I knew I needed to urge him on.

"I could really use some help with this." I said. "I am nearly finished with the invention and am anxious to get the raincoat protection paper J-Dad said I needed. Then no one can say it isn't mine."

Alex took another deep breath, hesitated a little, and said, "You could use the word 'vertical' for your 'V' position. That is the position I am in when I am begging for the Frisky Feline Fish Morsels. I stand in front of the bi-fold pantry room door on my hind paws, reach up with my front paws, and bang away on the door. Therefore, I am in a vertical position. Does that help you?"

Well, G-Ma, a bonafide real miracle had happened! I had just witnessed the manifestation of a midsummer night's dream about a chink in a wall; a chink in the heretofore, impenetrable, attitudinal wall that imprisons Alex's character flaw. The chink occurred right then and there! I remember my feline Mom telling me about some dead man named Shakespeare who had a wall and a chink. His chink and wall turned out to be a good thing for him too. Now we will be able to use the chink and gain access to Alex's character flaw. Hold on a minute! I hear a huge commotion outside. I'll get back to you as soon as possible.

Love,
Twitter

CHAPTER 17

The Chink in the Wall

Dear G-Ma,

The big ruckus last night went on until daylight. Shuggy barked and carried on as though there were robbers or bears attacking him. I watched out our front window, but all I ever saw was Shuggy running around and around the house. He came over to visit this morning, and I asked him about it. He said he makes a big commotion every once in a while for security reasons. Since he is a little guy like me, he said he has to bark very loudly to sound like a ferocious watchdog. He takes his security duties seriously too.

Last night I was telling you about the bonafide miracle. *As I see it,* Alex's offer to help was definitely a chink in his attitudinal wall. It hit me like a flash yesterday. It was as if a bright Edison flash bulb went on in my head. It was amazing! And I'm pretty sure I saw Alex's one, wide, up-bent whisker, which always points straight up to the twelve o'clock position, begin a quivering movement as it began to slowly bend downward. It stopped at approximately the twelve-ten o'clock position. The fatness of the whisker also seemed to melt away. It was obvious the whisker was destined to be on the straight and narrow like the rest of his whiskers. I even detected a lowering of the sneer on Alex's upper lip. If it continues, I'm sure his lip will turn into a nice smile.

His suggestion was wonderful. I thanked him and said, "The word 'vertical' for the 'V' in the title is perfect. Why don't you stay and watch me work on the actions? I want to get your 'vertical' suggestion absolutely correct."

He said, "No thank you Twitter. You'll be able to handle it without any help. I have something to do. If I'm lucky, our bathtub/laundry tub will have a hole in it soon."

JO ANN SPIESS, PH.D

I stared after Alex as he sashayed away. He was going to the laundry room to still try to stare a hole in our bathtub/ laundry tub. He really hates to take a bath in it. I can't say it is one of my favorite things to do either. In fact, *as I see it,* felines are perfectly capable of doing their own bathing. But L-Mom seems to think we need those soaking-all-over kinds of baths once in a while.

I sat there on the family room carpet and pondered the new turn of events. Now that the chink in Alex's attitudinal wall had occurred, we will all be able to slip through it with some much-needed help to change his character flaw. He had already exhibited a tremendous amount of change with the slight lowering of the up-bent whisker, and his offer to help with my invention. And then, all of a sudden, I realized Alex had also given me the answer to the action for the letter 'W'. He said he was going to the laundry room. That was a clear reference to the bathtub/ laundry tub. And that, in turn, was a reference to our baths. And that was a reference to the great amount of wiggling we have to do to shake the water off our fur before L-Mom towel dries us. Wasn't it clever of Alex to drop all those hints? It is amazing how things fall into place when you are not expecting them.

I squirmed all around on the carpet and began my warn-ups all over again. I worked very hard, and it took a lot of trials and errors before the actions and exact directions met with my approval. When the latest segment was finally finished, I called down the hall to Alex.

"Alex," I shouted, "would you like to see this? Thanks to you, it is now perfect."

When Alex came back around the hall corner and into the family room, as I had suggested, I knew the chink in his attitudinal wall was working.

"This is how it goes," I said. I then switched into my instructional voice and proceeded.

"Dear friends, you are about to learn the actions for the 'U-V-W' segment of the *Animal's Aerobic Alphabetical Actions* program. The 'U-V-W' is short for 'Ultimate Vertical Wiggle.' To begin, one stands on one's hind legs while up against the kitchen bi-fold pantry doors. If a kitchen pantry door is not available, one can pretend there is one, and substitute any other available door. One then extends one's front paws as high up as possible on the bi-fold doors. One is now positioned in the 'Ultimate Vertical' component of the action. One then begins a very vigorous body wiggle by moving one's body back and forth. This is akin to shaking bath water off one's entire body. This action exercises one's hips, abdominal area, and works one's upper pectorals. The action is done in conjunction with reciting the alphabet letters, 'U-V-W.' The action and accompanying recitations may be repeated as many times as one chooses."

"Well Alex," I said when finished, "what do you think? I even added 'dear friends' just for you."

Alex didn't say anything for a while. I was beginning to get worried. Had I offended him by using his obvious bathtub/ laundry tub reference? Surely he had meant to give me the wiggle hint for the 'W' action as he sashayed off to the laundry room. It was quite obviously a suggestion, *as I see it.*

I intently watched Alex for his reaction. He finally said, "It reminds me of something Marianne said to me once. I'll pass it along." He was smiling as he continued, "I think you really hit the nail on your head this time, Twitter."

"Thank you so much, Alex," I said, "I'm so glad you approve."

Well, G-Ma, my invention is nearly complete: Only one more segment to go. I need to keep at it while I'm on a roll, because our super-secret plans are all made and ready to take off. Won't everyone be surprised? I can hardly wait.

Inventing is very mentally and physically exhausting, so I decided to go out on the patio to take a break and do some abbreviated patrolling out there. It is a good thing I did, because as I approached the pool's screen door, I saw a little green lizard poking his head under the door. "Hey," I said. "What are you doing? You can't come in here. I don't allow lizards or anything else in here."

The little guy looked at me with his tiny beady eyes and said, "I just wanted to peek in here. It looks like a good place to find some ants. Do you have any ants you don't want?"

"There aren't any ants in here because I scared them all away. I didn't want them to get sucked up in L-Mom's vacuum cleaner as it zoomed around on the patio floor after their big party."

"Oh, well maybe I could find something else to eat in there," he said. "What about a fly? Are there any of those in there?"

"No, there are no flies in here either. They cause a great deal of trouble for me. Every once in a while, somehow, a fly will get in. The pesky thing will fly up high where I can't reach it. I have to be very patient and wait until it lands on something. Then I carefully sneak up and try to pounce on it. Sometimes it will see me in the middle of my pounce and fly away. When that happens, I have to start the process all over again. They fly from one room to the next and make a buzzing sound just to antagonize me. Sometimes I waste half a day before I can catch them. Sometimes I have to give up. And sometimes I later find them dead on a window sill."

The little lizard cocked his head at me and said, "Maybe I could come in and help you. I could sit extremely still. I am able to sit still for hours. I can even look as though I am dead. It is a technique of mine. Then the fly would come near me to see if I am good to eat, and quick as a flash, I could stick out my long tongue, capture it, and it would be gone! What do you think of that?"

I thought about his plan for a little bit. If I allowed him to come in here to live and catch flies, he might bring in his whole family. Suddenly I remembered my feline Mom telling me something about not letting a camel get his nose under my tent. I didn't have a tent, but I think Mom meant this exact situation. It seemed like a good place to change the subject.

"By the way," I asked, "do you know of a little green lizard that lost its tail in our family room?"

"Oh sure," he answered. "That was my cousin Loren Rosen. His name used to be longer, but he dropped the last letters. He's good at dropping things. Dropping his tail was a safety trick."

"That was a clever trick. Can you do any tricks?" I asked.

"Sure, I'll show you one."

With that, he raised his head and made the bottom of his throat puff way out. It was sort of a reddish color and it vibrated in and out. It was really weird! If he could do tricks like that, I thought it best to part ways with him and his whole clever family-especially Loren.

"No," I said, "I don't think I need any of your help, but thank you anyway. Besides, I have a strict rule about letting lizards into the patio. And here is another strict rule of mine. If one makes a rule it should be a good rule, and therefore one needs to stick to it, or something like that. So, you had better leave and tell your family my rules, especially your cousin Loren. He is the one who created such a disaster with L-Mom's sea shells.

"OK," he said as he backed out under the door. "Call me if you change your rules."

I was glad to see him go. It is my job, for the present time anyway, to keep security tight. I hurried back into the kitchen to get a little sip of my water and then into the family room to try to finish my invention.

All of a sudden I felt the need for a short catnap. Where was my warm sunny spot? "There you are!" I shouted as I spotted it halfway under the television. There was just enough of it sticking out on the carpet for me to stretch out and be comfortable.

It didn't take long for me to get refreshed, or so I thought. I was anxious to complete the invention so we could get on with our super-secret plans. I thought and thought and wiggled and wiggled on the carpet. Thinking is very tiring. Perhaps I didn't have a long enough catnap, because I was soon extremely tired. All at once I was aware of my whiskers signaling me to listen to my current situation. And then I had it! Like a lightening bolt in the blue it struck me. "Eureka!" I shouted, "I think I have found it: The perfect ending!"

The super exact words and the actions just flew into my head. As I lay on my warm sunny spot, I figuratively patted myself on the back.

"What are you doing, Twitter?" Alex said as he came back into the family room.

I was in my most comfortable position of all as I looked up at him and said, "Alex, I just finished the perfect kind of ending for my invention."

"Let me see it," he said.

I continued to hold down my warm sunny spot on the carpet as I went into my authoritative voice to recite the directions, as they will be written. "Dear friends, this is the 'X-Y-Z' segment of your *Animal's Aerobic Alphabetic Actions* program, commonly called *Twitter's Triple A*. This is the only segment for which one does not need to do any warm-ups. This action is titled 'Xercising Your Zs.' One gets in the most comfortable position possible. One then drifts off to sleep, simultaneously exercising one's throat with many Z sounds. These sounds are somewhat akin to a soft snoring-like purr. One then visualizes all the previous positions, thereby getting one's virtual exercise in addition to practicing the aforementioned alphabet. This segment is designed to refresh one's body while solidifying the actions and alphabetic letters to one's memory. One cannot overdo this segment."

"Well, Alex," I asked, "what do you think?"

"Twitter," he said, "it's obvious you put a lot of effort into your invention, so I'm not going to spoil it by pointing out you used the letter 'A' four times in the title, but only three times in the common title of *Twitter's Triple A.*"

"That is very kind of you Alex," I said. I didn't know what he was talking about when he mentioned a misspelling, but I think it had to be some kind of compliment.

Well, G-Ma, I appreciated Alex's kind words. The chink in his attitudinal wall is certainly allowing us to slip through and favorably influence his character flaw. And now that my invention is perfected, J-Dad can send for the raincoat protection paper for it. My next project is a difficult one: Informing L-Mom and J-Dad about our super- secret plans. It has been very hard to keep our plans from them. They will be surprised and happy for us, I hope. And maybe they will be a little sad too. I'll get started on it tomorrow night when they are asleep.

Love,
Twitter

CHAPTER 18

The Super-Secret

Dear G-Ma, this is what I left in the computer.
Dear L-Mom & J-Dad,

You were probably very surprised this morning when you came out of your bedroom and there were no toys on the floor for you to pick up. I knew you would both be worried when all you could find of me was an old hairball or two. Well, G-Ma and I discussed it for quite some time and we decided to give you a big surprise. You see, G-Ma and I have had an exciting super-secret for a while. I also knew one of you would check your e-mail sometime during the day. You would then find this letter. It explains the whole story about our exciting super-secret. Alex has been sworn to secrecy since I told him, and he is all excited about it too.

As you know, animals and creatures live in the present. They cannot think about their future. Somehow I was given super- danger whiskers which have insight into the future. They have alerted me to coming dangers ever since I was a tiny kitten. My super-danger whiskers have also taught me to think and see beyond the present. They have always guided my actions by pointing me in the right direction. And they have urged me to make the decision which you are about to read. It is as though my destiny was planned when I was born. What I'm trying to say is this. I have made some super-secret plans with G-Ma. We did it all under the cover so you wouldn't find out about it. We were terribly afraid you would get worried and try to stop our secret adventure. G-Ma was certain you would not want her to leave the place where she lives with just me to help guide her. She wants you to know her driver's license card is still in good shape.

You see, I learned how to use our computer all by myself during the down times of my nighttime patrolling. It was a little frustrating at first, but now the computer is another one of my friends. So now, with our computer's help, I send G-Ma an e-mail letter nearly every night. She likes to know what goes on with the rest of her family at our house. G-Ma learned a little bit about sending e-mails too. A nice lady, named Amanda, who works at the home where G-Ma lives, taught her how to do e-mails. She doesn't send me e-mails very often because all that technical stuff is still a little confusing for her. When she has a pinch though, she can do it. Usually her return e-mails only contain the day's dining room menu and all the current ailments and latest maladies of her friends. I am careful to delete her responses. We don't want that kind of personal information to cause trouble for anyone.

It seems the residents where she lives don't sleep well at night and G-Ma is no exception. For some reason they all have their days and nights mixed up. G-Ma said she thinks it has something to do with their age; like losing their hair, and teeth, and a lot of other things. So every night at midnight she goes down to a room where there are a lot of computers, and she watches for my letters to come through the air.

G-Ma took a naming idea from my *Animal's Aerobic Alphabetic Actions* invention. She named her nightgown trek to the computer room the *3-M*. It is short for *The Midnight Mail Maneuver*.

G-Ma printed out all of my e-mails and took them back to her room. Rereading them during the daytime makes her happy and helps her remember what I wrote. She says it also makes her feel as though she is right here with us. Rereading also helps her drop into nice long daytime catnaps.

One day a lady came to conduct a project for the residents at G-Ma's place. The lady said everyone should call her "Project Bobi" because her job was to have people do her projects. She told them she had the perfect project for all of them to do. They were supposed to write down everything they could remember about their lives from the very beginning to this exact day. Her project was supposed to be good for their health or something like that.

G-Ma didn't have much writing experience so she had a little talk with Project Bobi. G-Ma explained her lack of writing ability and said she was so sorry she wouldn't be able to do the project. And besides, there wasn't anything about her life that anyone would want to read.

Project Bobi told her she shouldn't be so modest and not to hide her bushel under a light. G-Ma still didn't want to do the assigned project, so she came up with a better idea. She told Project Bobi she had a grandcat that wrote interesting e-mails to her nearly every night at midnight, and she could use those for her project.

For some reason, Project Bobi didn't believe, first of all, that G-Ma even had a grandcat, and second of all, that a cat could send e-mail letters to her. Well, G-Ma got her pretty blue-tinted hair all ruffled and said to Project Bobi, "*Wait just one darn minute!*"

She then huffed out of the meeting room and slowly trotted off to her own tiny room to get all my e-mail letters from under her bed. Two nice young maintenance men named Manuel and Liam helped her cut down an old thrown away cardboard box from the trash room to make it fit under her low bed. The bed has to be low to the floor so she can get in and out of it easily. It is also a safety feature, because if she did fall out, she wouldn't have far to fall.

When G-Ma returned to the meeting room, the other residents were busily writing about their lives. She got Project Bobi's attention and showed her the old cut-down cardboard box with all my e-mail letters. Some of them were not in very good shape anymore. They were quite worn from all the rereading and some had tea stains and cookie crumbs stuck to them. Well, Project Bobi was shocked when she looked at several of my e-mails. She didn't seem to mind all the tea stains and cookie crumbs because when she finished reading she said, "This is fantastic! The world needs to see the treasure you had hidden in your old cut-down cardboard box."

G-Ma was still a little peeved with Project Bobi. She said, "These e-mail letters were definitely not hidden. They were right there in the cut-down cardboard box under my bed. All anyone had to do was look under my bed." She also said it was an obvious fact that there was no other place to keep them in her tiny apartment, and everyone should be able to grasp that concept very easily.

G-Ma sent me an e-mail about all of it and said she didn't think Project Bobi heard any of her huffy words, and maybe it was just as well, because Project Bobi was so happy and excited. The only thing Project Bobi had on her mind was to quickly leave the meeting room and get to her car with G-Ma's old cut-down cardboard box filled with my tea stained, cookie crumbed, reread e-mail letters.

Well, L-Mom and J-Dad, events happened rapidly after Project Bobi left with the box. She soon contacted G-Ma and told her she worked for some company that knew how to do lots of good stuff with tea stained, cookie crumbed, reread e-mail letters. The nice company wanted to publish my e-mail letters into a real book. The company also said the tea stains and cookie crumbs didn't make a hoot of difference. The publishing company also sent G-Ma a lot of money to set up an account for us, and they said we had to go on a cross country book signing tour right now. I was so shocked you could have knocked me off my socks!

The bad part of the whole deal is that we have to leave Naples for a little while. After we go on the cross country book signing tour, we will eventually end up in California. A good part of the deal is that we have decided to search for the lady who has the back porch where I was born. I would like to ask her to if she knows where my feline Mom and littermates Gomer and Harold now live. I also want to tell Mom I'm sorry I can't exactly remember all the things she told me to remember. But I think I do a pretty good job of remembering the most important parts.

I had a long talk with Alex about my new adventure as a book signer. He said if my shoe was on the other foot he would do the same thing. Alex is coming along very well with improving his character flaw. We also talked about his advancement to head of my security patrolling. I showed him the rigid schedule he would have to keep, my rules, and where to look for the trouble spots. He also had to be taught how to deal with critters who want to come into the house or get on the patio for some made-up reason. He was actually eager to take over all his new duties. He even had a tiny smile on his face.

We also had a long talk about the bathtub/laundry tub. I told him he was wasting his efforts by trying to stare a hole in it, because I had already tried, and it didn't work. I also told him the best thing to do when L-Mom insists on a full soaking bath in that dreaded laundry tub is to go into a yoga-like trance. I actually taught him how to do it. Which reminds me, now that my healthful and educational *Animal's Aerobic Alphabetic Actions* program is finished, and J-Dad is getting the raincoat protection paper for it, I have started writing an exciting seagull to it. It is a relaxation yoga program. Alex was proud to be the first one ever to learn one of the new yoga actions. I'll be very busy trying to work on it while signing all my books, but it will help to keep my mind tack-sharp.

Alex, of course, had to know about our super-secret so he could have his advancement to head of the security patrolling. He promised to keep quiet about it. He seemed happy for me and even helped with my upcoming getaway. He said to me, "I know every nook and cranny in the laundry room since I spend so much time in there. I have the perfect way for you to sneak out of the house."

"Tell me quickly Alex, tell me." I urged him on.

"You don't know it, but the small window in the laundry room is always open a little bit for fresh air, and the screen is loose in one corner. I'm surprised you never notice it. That is probably how the black beetle got in. I remember you telling me about him. You know; the one whose legs flew off when you were batting him around."

The security breech was a complete shock to me. I said, "Yeah, I remember the silly little guy. I never thought about patrolling the window sills. You will have to add that to your temporary promotion to security chief. Thank you for providing the answer for my departure."

"If you jump up on the ledge, you will see that the screen is not very secure at all and could easily be pushed out. All you would have to do is give it a little shove and it would go sailing through the air to the ground. And your skinny little body would easily squeeze under the window. Then you could jump out. I discovered all about it shortly after I moved here and was thinking about escaping."

I thanked him very kindly and then asked him to explain to Shuggy, all my bird friends, and our lime tree, exactly what the new change would be since he was temporarily advanced to head of security patrolling. I also asked him to keep Shuggy, and all the rest of my good friends, informed about all the happenings concerning my book signing trip. He can get the information from the e-mails which G-Ma and I will send on our new fancy Windows 10 laptop computer. I also loaned him my warm sunny spots on the family room carpet.

Whoops, I think I hear G-Ma in the driveway now. If I'm just hearing things, I'll be right back to tell you all the rest of our super-secret. If it really is G-Ma in the driveway, you will get an e-mail tomorrow night from wherever we are on the road.

Love,
Twitter

CHAPTER 19

The Preparations

Dear L-Mom & J-Dad,

Nope, the noise was just my anticipation, I guess, so I'll tell you all the rest of our super- secret planning. As I said earlier, the nice company making my book sent G-Ma a check which they called "advance money." She said the company must have made a big mistake, because in her book, (she really doesn't have a book); the word "advance" means some money is given before the rest of the money is given. In this case, they never gave her any earlier money before they sent the advance check. G-Ma thought it all over and told me she decided to keep the money, because she did not want to embarrass the company by bringing the error to their attention.

We did some more super-secret planning after we had the advance check. I wasn't very good at some of it, because I had to plan my actions for the book signings, photo ops, my new yoga invention, and maybe even a travel guide. G-Ma said she had a black belt in shopping, so she would buy all the things we needed. I still don't understand why anyone would need a black belt to go shopping, but I'm glad she has one.

The actual shopping created a problem for a little while until G-Ma had an excellent idea. She has a very good friend named Mr. Jay, whose job is to just sit behind the desk all night at the place where she lives. He is supposed to answer the phone if any of the residents can't sleep and they need someone to talk with them. A lot of times, no one calls him and he gets bored. Then he either goes down the hall to the theater room to put on a movie, or he calls G-Ma and they chat for a long time about a lot of things. She said he is very knowledgeable about all the important stuff in life. When she told him about our book signing trip, the need to go shopping, and the misnamed advance check, he offered to help us with anything and everything we would need.

G-Ma thanked him very kindly and accepted his help. His first helpful act was to be at her door early the next morning. He helped her into his car and they headed for downtown Naples.

Mr. Jay said, "You will have to give the bank president that big misnamed advance money check, and then we all will be smelling in the clover." G-Ma said that sounded good to her.

When they got to the bank, the bank president said, "There has to be two signatures on this account ma'am, who else do you want to have access to the account?"

Mr. Jay said he would be glad to help by adding his name to the account. G-Ma took him up on his offer. She said she knew he was honest, and strictly on the level, even though she knew he was just a tiny bubble off plumb. The president of the bank gave them a check book after they both signed something. G-Ma said it didn't look like any book she had ever seen, but she took the book anyway, and kindly thanked the bank president. Later she told me that there must be a lot of people writing all kinds and shapes of books.

The next thing they had to do was buy a car for us.

Mr. Jay said, "I know where you can get a steal at Carl Chew's Classy Cars." Then he drove her there to get our steal.

G-Ma told me she said, "I certainly don't want to steal anything!" Mr. Jay assured her she was in good hands with his friend, the used car dealer. He also assured her no one would break any laws or steal anything on this deal.

G-Ma told him we needed a heavy duty car with a lot of room and a big spare tire. She didn't want any of those little donut tires, because if a tire wore out, we would have to use the silly thing. She worried that the donut tire wouldn't last long enough if we were stuck out in the desert somewhere and still had a long way to drive to get to California.

She looked at all of Carl's classy used cars when they got there and settled on a Buick Regal convertible. I was happy about the convertible part. It will allow me to see in all directions. It will be much better than my dreaded cave-like cat carrier that I have to use to go to our vet's office. They had to leave our new used car at Carl Chew's Classy Cars place for a few days so Carl could pump up the tires a little better and wash the windshield. G-Ma then tore out the first page of the bank president's book. Both G-Ma and Mr. Jay signed it and then gave it to Carl.

Their next stop was an auto supply store. They were shopping for a car seat for me. She told me there is a Florida law stating, "Everyone sitting in the front passenger seat of any car has to wear a seat belt." It is a very silly law, *as I see it!* If I had to have a seat belt on me, it would be like a strait jacket and it would probably strangle me. The auto supply store didn't have anything suitable, so G-Ma and Mr. Jay were sent to the Pets R Yours store.

The pet store people found just the right seat for me. It hooks over the back of the front passenger seat, has the needed seatbelt, and has a big pocket across the front. The pocket is big enough to hold Billy Two and some cookies for G-Ma. I will even be able to put in a few Frisky Feline Fish Morsels for me. It is important to take some morsel snacks for me, because they are a big part of my food pyramid.

The last place G-Ma and Mr. Jay went to was a Better Buy store. They wanted to find a geek who would sell them a computer. They were lucky because one was standing right by the entrance door as they walked in.

"Welcome," he said, "I'm Bob, by-golly, Carrigan. There are ten salesmen in the geek squad here in this store. You are very lucky because I am the top geek. I sell people things and later I fix them. I can fix anything you buy from me. Did you notice my car outside? On the side it says, 'GEEK SQUAD.' I will use it to come to your home to fix any purchase you make today. Now, what item would you proudly like to take home today?"

"Well, Bob by-golly," said G-Ma, "that sounds very honorable. We want to buy a computer. I will be sure to keep in touch with you all the way to California so you will know where to come if we need any fixing."

Bob, by-golly, was very confused about us not having a home where he could come to fix whatever we bought until he was told the entire story. Then he said, "I have oodles of computers. A laptop is exactly what you need for the trip because it is portable."

G-Ma told him her grandcat would be the one using the computer and he had a very small lap. Therefore, it would have to be a very small laptop.

Bob, by golly, said he knew exactly what the answer was to the lap problem, because solving problems was his job. He said he was the best geek at the store for solving problems and that is why he was the top geek. He then told G-Ma she should buy one of his big wonderful Windows 10 laptops. He said it was the latest model and a lot of people were updating to it. He also said a lot people didn't like some of the features, but those people should not have bought it in the first place. He went on to say he was sure her grandcat was smart enough to figure it all out. G-Ma said she really liked the top geek after he said that about me.

"What you need to do," he went on, "is put the computer on your lap, have your grandcat sit close, and use his tail to swipe the fancy screen. Your grandcat can also use one paw for the keys, and not have to bother about using the misnamed mouse gadget."

Mr. Jay said she should buy it, so she tore another page from the bank president's book and gave it to the geek. All our purchasing preparations were then completed.

Project Bobi, from the publishing company, contacted G-Ma last week and told her she wants me to send e-mails to you about our search for my feline Mom and littermates, Gomer and Harold. I am also to send e-mails about all the hotels, motels, photo-ops, book signings, and everything else we do on this trip. She wants me to send them every night until we get to California. She wants you to print my e-mails and give her clean copies of them. The tea stained and cookie crumbed e-mails were okay, but the publishing company prefers clean copies.

Project Bobi said she was going to publish them all and make more books. She is going to call them my seagull books. G-Ma said Project Bobi had better be careful or she would be putting the horse in the cart if she publishes a seagull book before my first book is published.

When our cross country trip is finished, I am also to continue to write about our great adventure with Mr. Jay. Then Project Bobi will make another seagull book.

I saved this part of our plan for last. It is so exciting! Once we finish the book-signing stuff and make all that money, we will meet Mr. Jay in California. He wanted us to hire him as a body guard during our big trip so he could protect us from the paparazzi and also to protect the checkbook. G-Ma told him we could take very good care of ourselves and the checkbook. Then Mr. Jay made all the plans for some great adventures for all of us when we get to California.

It seems as though Mr. Jay had been thinking of taking a leave from his nighttime desk job anyway, because Mr. Diamond told him he couldn't watch movies all night in the theater. I guess he was answering the resident's phone calls on his cell phone instead of using the phone at the front desk. Mr. Diamond told him that henceforth, Mr. Jay was to stay at the front desk all night and do his answering from there. Mr. Jay told him the desk chair was too hard, and it was not comfortable enough for long catnaps. *As I see it,* long catnaps are essential to one's health and well-being. Apparently Mr. Jay's last statement was the straw that broke Mr. Diamond's back, because now Mr. Jay is going to meet us in California.

He said we are to hook up again in California where he will take on the job of volunteer body guard. He said we definitely will need protection for all the book money and the annoying paparazzi out there. He also legally changed his name for some reason. We are to call him "Biker Dude" now, because he will be driving his fancy bright orange 1993 Harley Davidson 90th Anniversary, FX soft-tail motorcycle. I am going to sit on the leather pouch behind the handlebars where my paws can get a good grip. G-Ma will be comfortable sitting behind Mr. Jay and hanging tight to his leather jacket. He is also going to take off the windshield so the wind will blow through my hair. Then we will all go whizzing up and down the highways. He also has plans for a 3 1/2 hour ride to Las Vegas. He is going to teach us how to do the gambling stuff there. I will be sure to e-mail you all about that great adventure. Project Bobi may want to use that also for another seagull book for me.

Alex asked where we were going to sleep tomorrow night. I'm glad he is worried about us.

I reassuringly told him G-Ma picked out a really tall hotel so we could see a long way off out our windows.

He smiled and said, "Well be careful, because you know your elevator doesn't go all the way to the top."

I thanked him for the advice and said I was sure G-Ma would be happy for the information.

Oh! Oh! Alex has been watching out the front window for me. I devised two secret signals for us. When he sees G-Ma's car coming up the driveway, he is supposed to start singing, "On the Road Again." I think I hear him singing it now, so I must shut down this computer and run to the laundry room. Then I will jump up on the window, push the broken screen open enough for me to jump out, land in the wet grass, and give Alex my next secret signal. I have borrowed a line from Shakespeare for my second signal. This is what I am going to do. I will shout up to Alex, "Romeo! Romeo! Wherefore are you Art?" I learned that from a television program. Alex will then throw Billy Two out the window to me and I will catch him. Then G-Ma will help me get settled in my new legal car seat, and away we will go. Wish us well. I promise to buy souvenirs and to e-mail every little detail to you about my new life's happenings. Then you can give them to Project Bobi for my seagull books.

Oh! I forgot. Don't worry about us because G-Ma promised to drive very slowly all the way to California.

Love,
Twitter

Ft. Myers Police Arrest Form

Date   20-July   **Time**   12:24 AM

Arresting Officer   Sgt. James Perrill

Location   Interstate Rest Stop

Offense Committed   Illegally In The Weeds

Name Of Arrestee   Twitter   Race   Feline

Gender M/F   Male   Age   5

Place Of Birth   The nice lady's house.

Current Address   None

Last Known Address   L-Mom and J-Dad's House

Arrestee's Demeanor At Time Of Arrest:
> Twitter was cooperative but seemed to have
> something on his mind.

Statements Made By Arrestee:
> When asked why he was illegally in the weeds he
> said, "I want a Lawyer!"

Arresting Officer's Comments:
> Twitter was traveling with a lady known only as G-Ma.
> When asked where he was going he said, "To California to meet
> biker Dude." This was confirmed by the lady known only as
> G-Ma. When Twitter was put in the squad car and asked if he
> had any further comments he said, "I want a Lawyer!"

EPILOGUE

Twitter swishes his tail across his new laptop, uses one paw, and begins to type.

Dear L-Mom and J-Dad,

We didn't even get as far as Ft. Myers!! And it's only 25 miles away!

G-Ma and I were doing very well for just a short while. We were minding our own business and, as I promised, we were driving very slowly. I guess all the excitement affected me, because all of a sudden I started to wiggle and wiggle. G-Ma recognized my symptoms, so she pulled way off to the side of the road and into some tall weeds. We both got out and walked a little way into the tall wet weeds. All of a sudden a policeman drove up behind us. He sat in his car for a little while and then strutted close to where we were standing. It was too dark for him to see me in the tall weeds, but he could see G-Ma. He began talking with her and asking silly questions. I overheard the entire conversation and will now tell you the whole sordid mess.

The haughty policeman said, "Ma'am, where are you going?"

G-Ma answered, "We are going to California, and my relative will sign books on the way."

"I noticed you were driving extremely slowly, Ma'am. Can you explain why?"

"Of course," said G-Ma, "we promised our family that we would be extra cautious and driving slowly is being extra cautious."

"Well, that's a new one," he said.

I thought the policeman must have been one brick short of a load if he couldn't grasp that simple concept.

The tall weeds were wet and cold, and I was getting more and more uncomfortable just standing there. I was wishing he would go away and arrest some bad guys. We needed to continue on with our business trip and great California adventure.

"Okay, so what are you doing way over here in the weeds?" he asked.

Not wanting to embarrass me, G-Ma was very hesitant to say anything. Then she very cleverly said, "I had to stretch my legs. Do you know anything about arthritis, sir?"

The patrolman didn't answer the question. He simply carried on with another question as he asked, "Ma'am, may I see your driver's license?"

"Certainly," G-Ma said cheerfully.

If the sock would have been on the other foot, G-Ma would have been up to *her* ears in the wet weeds and *I* would have been talking to the policeman. I know I would not have been as cheerful as she was.

She left me standing there with the tall weeds over my head and went back to our car to get her driving card. She searched in her huge purse, found the card, and gave it to the policeman.

The policeman shined his flashlight on the card and said, "Ma'am, this card is no good."

"Young man," G-Ma said.

I knew by her tone she was getting a little upset with the policeman and, *as I see it,* she had every reason to be upset. He was wasting our time and could not comprehend what was going on.

"That is a perfectly good card," G-Ma said, "it is in good shape. It doesn't have one wrinkle. Furthermore, my card does not have any tea stains or anything else on it."

The policeman told her something about the driving card coming to its end. I didn't think he was making much sense at all. How on earth could a card come to an end?

"Where did you say you were going?" he asked again.

"Young man," G-Ma said indignantly, "I already told you we are going to California."

"To do what?" he continued.

"After we sign books, my relative and I are going to ride on a motorcycle."

I was very proud of G-Ma by this time. She was pretty much keeping her cool and answering all those silly questions. I, on the other hand, was still standing in the tall wet weeds and getting more and more uncomfortable.

"What relative?" he asked, "I don't see any relative. What is your relative's name?"

"His name is Twitter," G-Ma said. I could tell she was now getting very exasperated.

"Twitter? Twitter what?" he demanded.

G-Ma hesitated a few minutes, smiled, and finally said, "It's the same as our whole family: my sons, their wives, and mine. Therefore, it would *have* to be Spiess."

The answer to that question should have been obvious, *as I see it!"*

Well, L-Mom and J-Dad, I was extremely nervous standing off the road in those tall weeds. I could clearly hear every word and my night vision eyes were able to see through the breaks in the weeds. I assure you, G-Ma was still calm and holding her own with the pesky policeman.

"Ma'am," the policeman said, "would you be willing to take a little test?"

"What kind of test?"

"It is a very simple test. All you have to do is walk in a straight line."

I wondered if the silly policeman thought people walked in a sideways line. It certainly was a strange request. He was just wasting our time and aggravating us. We had important things to do and exciting places to go. Besides, we badly needed to get on with what I was doing in the weeds.

The policeman told G-Ma to walk a short bit in a straight line down the road. She did exactly as he told her to do. She walked very slowly, as usual, and wobbled a bit because of her arthritis, but I thought she did fine.

"Ma'am, you can come back now. Have you been drinking?" he asked.

"Yes, of course!" G-Ma replied. "All my doctors stress the need to keep my body hydrated."

There was a lot more of their silly conversation, and then I heard the policeman say something about going to the police station. After more conversation, they both came over to where I was standing.

The flashlight finally found me and the policeman said, "What are you doing in those tall weeds?"

I was rightly perturbed. I should have shouted to him, "I forgot to bring my litterbox!"

The pesky policeman made us get into the back seat of his car. He fiddled around with a phone and lots of dials. Then he turned around and said, "Ma'am, the two of you have a lot of legal problems. Apparently you don't know what 'expired' means and the Collier County Animal Services reports Twitter's tags are in question.

Events happened pretty fast after that. We got to the station and had to answer even sillier questions. They took away G-Ma's pretty pink necklace, her tiny gold ring, and her big purse. She told them her big purse had important stuff in it: the bank president's book. And she said she needed to guard it very carefully. The policeman took it away from her anyway. They said they would protect it from robbers and bad guys until they sorted out our situation. G-Ma put up another fuss when they tried to take away our laptop computer too. She said, "That is a brand new Windows 10 laptop. It hasn't even been used yet. A lot of people can't figure out how to use it, but my grandcat is smart and all he will have to do is swish his tail over the screen and marvelous things will happen. And furthermore, he has to send e-mails through the air every night."

All the policemen at the station looked at each other and sent some kind of secret signals to each other. Then one of them said, "We should write a book about this one!"

It seems as though everyone is writing books.

Then a lady policeman came into the room and said, "Follow me."

I was beginning to have big tears in my eyes, but I think the name on her badge was N.Tippy-Topp. It seemed like a strange name for such a pretty lady policewoman.

She took us to another room where she had a messy inky thing and she finger and paw printed us. Then a different policeman took us down a long hallway to a small cubical. Three of its sides were gray concrete walls and the front of it had metal bars all over it. We went into the cubical and the policeman locked the door. Very slowly we walked to the bunk beds and sat down on the lower bunk. I think I could have squeezed out through the bars, but I didn't want to leave G-Ma all alone. She needed me to protect and advise her. Thank goodness they put us in the same cubicle!

G-Ma held me in her nice big lap and began petting me. I'm sure I could feel teardrops falling down on my fur. It made my own big teardrops fall too. After a while, between sniffles, I said to G-Ma, "How in the world will J-Dad and L-Mom ever find us?"

G-Ma thought a bit before answering and said, "It will be very easy Twitter. You left paw prints from the fingerprint ink all over the floor of the police station, and they lead directly down the hall to our cubicle." G-Ma is so wise.

Love,
Twitter

Twitter begins to shut down his new laptop computer and suddenly stops! Smiles replace his tears when a message flashes on his screen with these words: "YOU HAVE MAIL!"